THE HALLOWEEN CHAMBER
CHAMBER
Revenge of the Corvids

The Halloween Chamber

Grimsfell 'neath Oros

For Matthew & Louise,
Alexander & Eleanor

THE HALLOWEEN CHAMBER
Revenge of the Corvids

Richard E Harding

The Halloween Chamber

Font in Palatino Linotype 11 pt

ISBN 978-0-9574159-5-9

A CIP catalogue record for this book is available from the British Library

Written, formatted, edited, published and cover design
by Richard E Harding B.Sc. (Hons) Biol, Geol.

CONTENTS

The Halloween Chamber

Lovers' Crag

INTRODUCTION

About This Book

Afters completing my first two books I needed an idea for another, and then, one day I heard some crows outside producing their ominous distinctive calls. This set me thinking about the crow and raven family of corvids and their remarkable intelligence.

Being a fan of Gothic architecture I instinctively linked the corvids, especially the ravens, to be inhabiting an enormous Gothic cathedral. Gargoyles and bats entered my mind-scape as additional characters and I concocted a story about four gargoyles who had figured out how to escape their centuries of entrapment within the stonework at the edge of the towering cathedral's roof, with the aid of lubricating rain and determined wriggling!

Once free, this jolly bunch of fellows go on to explore the vast roof, meeting the resident bat family on their travels and hear about the evil ravens who dominate the building in their threatening manner.

This was going to have to be a children's story the way it was going and I found it difficult to continue without the descriptions becoming too scary, demonic and evil sounding.

The Halloween Chamber

I *wanted* to go that route with new ideas popping-up thick and fast, so I abandoned the story and wrote a new beginning which would eventually meet up with my more occult demonic ideas to continue the new story.

The cathedral was reinvented as an ancient abbey on a remote Scottish coast with a history of strange activity involving the monks and the people of the little village of Grimsfell 'neath Oros, a huge, double-peaked limestone mountain, from *oros*, the ancient Greek word for mountain.

A professor of psychiatry is employed by the abbot to try and solve a centuries-old problem affecting his monks, concerning three ravens and a crow, some witches, a few Germans, a demon or two and a strange, potent and intelligent miasmic fluid called Vril. The story starts in 1953 when I was seven years old, and eight years after World War Two had ended. I was born at mid-day on 31st October 1946 !

I hope you enjoy my story which unfolded gradually as I wrote and edited it - even I didn't know what was to happen next! I also changed the cover texts and images many times before I was satisfied. Apologies for any remaining mistakes that have defied my rigorous scrutiny.

I plan to finish the children's story and have accompanying illustrations to bring the characters to life.

Richard E Harding – April 2016

CHAPTER ONE

Arrival

One cold, rainy, blustery November night, a lone figure stood illuminated by a single light from beyond the large ornate abbey gates. The sound of the taxi receded into the night as he put down his heavy bag with a sigh, pleased at last to have arrived at his destination.

Grimsfell Abbey stood imposingly high above the bleak coastline, overlooking the little village tucked in amongst a few leaning windswept trees. The hills behind the abbey gave way to the ever-increasing slope of scrub-land up to the vast limestone mountain that dominated the landscape. He could feel the presence of the mountain even though he could not see it, as he blinked in the direction of the little light directing him to the entrance.

After moving the heavy iron gate just enough to squeeze through, Professor Benson made his way up the weed-infested crunching gravel path towards the light above a small doorway partially hidden by stunted cypress trees. He wiped away the drops of rain from his face and tugged the cast iron bell-pull handle, which responded with a faint tinkle from behind the oak door. After a while the door creaked open to reveal a small man in a monk's habit staring up at him. It was the middle of the night and the professor immediately apologised for arriving at such a late hour, explaining how he was held up at the nearest town trying to find a taxi that could take him this far into the rain-lashed night.

The diminutive monk said that he was expected and that a room had been made ready for him. That was exactly what the professor needed - a good rest. Hot tea and biscuits were rustled up for him and the little monk bade him goodnight and said he would inform the abbot of his arrival in the morning.

It was late morning by the time the professor was awakened by a knock on his door.

"Hello there. I'm sorry to wake you, but just to pass on a message from abbot Gregory," came the little monk's voice. "He will see you at two thirty in his study."

"OK, thanks."

"Would you like some breakfast – toast and tea?"

"That would be wonderful," replied the professor. "I'll be down soon."

Professor Benson was no stranger to investigating unexplained occurrences and the people involved, especially events of a paranormal nature. He was a tall middle-aged man, softly spoken, who dressed conservatively in a suit and waistcoat, set off by a bow tie. The day was in stark contrast to the night before, with the sun threatening its way through the thinning cloud. The wind and rain had all but ceased and some birds were pleasantly singing. The professor paused by his window to admire the view on his way out to the passageway to find the bathroom. His window faced the sloping landscape down to the cliffs and the sea with the little village of Grimsfell nestled in a hollow to his right, between the abbey and the cliff-tops.

After successfully navigating the passages beyond his room he discovered a quaint, white-tiled bathroom with the yellowing white enamelled iron bath supported on clawed feet, complete with a set of large, industrial looking brass taps. The ancient cast-iron cistern above his head whistled with leaking water pressure with that irritating sound which is only eliminated for a brief time by activating the clanking mechanism - a first-time flush achieved by trial and error and deft manipulation of the chain pull.

Cream coloured bath and hand towels were neatly displayed upon matching brass rails beside the robust rectangular hand-basin, together with a new bar of coal-tar soap, flannel and a floral porcelain tooth mug seated in a wall-mounted brass ring. After a much anticipated wash, he found his way back along the passages to his room, only to be surprised on turning the corner to be confronted by an agitated chanting monk, clasping and unclasping his hands in rhythmic fashion.

"I'm sorry, I nearly bumped into you there," apologised the professor. But the monk seemed oblivious to his presence and shuffled on past him down the corridor in the direction of the bathroom. Something was troubling him.

After his late breakfast in a small room next to the dining hall, the professor lay on his bed acclimatising himself to his new surroundings, and at the appointed time was downstairs in the oak-panelled hallway and began to admire the paintings on the wall panels, except *admire* wasn't really the word to use. They were disturbing paintings with a distinct theme to them - fear, persecution, suffering, pain and death.

His deep concentration on the detail of the paintings was broken by the sudden voice of a man standing at the far end of the hallway.

"Professor Benson. So good of you to come and see us. I hope you had a good night after your arrival in all that wind and rain. I'm afraid the weather up here can be quite intense at times."

"Well it certainly was last night, but I had a very welcome rest, thank you," responded the professor walking towards him. "I understand from your letter that you have an urgent need for some advice and guidance concerning some of your monk's strange behaviour, abbot."

"Indeed. Please come along to my study and I'll attempt to explain the situation," said the abbot, gesticulating in the direction of his room. To one side of the hallway stood a magnificent potted aspidistra plant displayed on an ornate, elevated plinth, the whole structure standing taller than its frequent admirers.

Once inside, the abbot closed the door behind them and walked across the large oaken study.

"Please would you excuse me for a moment?" the abbot asked without looking up, as he opened a small door to another room, pausing to place a hand on his forehead.

"Of course. I'll have a look around your splendid room if I may."

Quite a long time passed and the professor was concerned, moving to outside the closed door.

"Excuse me abbot, but are you all right in there?"

Receiving no reply, he waited for a while before partially opening the door to call again.

"Hello! Are you OK?"

Professor Benson put his head around the door to see the

abbot sitting on a chair in the small room. He was quietly sobbing.

"Oh! I'm *so* sorry. I was worried you might not have been feeling well," he explained. The abbot looked embarrassed.

"You could say that," he said. "I haven't been able to sleep much at all lately. I'm sorry to have lost my composure like this, but I'm so glad you've arrived here to try and help us."

"You must tell me what on earth is going on here. Can I get you something – a drink perhaps?"

"No, no, I'll be fine once I've explained the troubles here."

The professor went back into the study and sat on one of the richly upholstered carved chairs. The abbot emerged after a minute or so to sit at his desk, his shaking hands clasped over his face in apparent despair, eventually looking up at the professor.

"I took up the position here eight years ago, and at first all was well and I was very much looking forward to the challenges of my new job here at the abbey. At the beginning of the next New Year I became aware that some of my brother monks were displaying rather odd behaviour."

"*Odd* behaviour?" repeated the professor.

"Well, I didn't think much of it at first, but I became increasingly aware that a few of the brothers I had come to know quite well, seemed offish and kind of detached. Later, two of them barely spoke to me and spent long hours in their rooms instead of attending to their duties. I eventually had to call them to my office to enquire about their problems. It was then I knew something was terribly wrong.

"Brother Gilbert was the first. He sat in the chair you are now sitting in, with what I can only describe as a grimace upon his face – a kind of smug, self-satisfied, distorted grin. When I began to question him he wouldn't look directly at me and what followed shocked me greatly. He began chanting blasphemy, using strange hand gestures to emphasise his words. All I can say is that it was pure evil to watch him. It mattered not what I said, he remained in this bizarre animated state, only to end when I asked him to leave and seek advice from our physician. He left the room without a word, leaving the door wide open."

"He obviously had some mental problem. What happened after that?"

"He disappeared from the abbey. Despite many hours searching, I eventually contacted the police in the town and they conducted a missing persons' search, but to no avail – he simply seemed to vanish. He wasn't the only one.

"While all this was going on another brother asked to see me and we began to talk. At first he said he was having trouble sleeping and was experiencing disturbing nightmares, which he explained were difficult to tell from reality. He would wake suddenly in terrible fear and be unable to quickly realise it was a bad dream. He told me he was embarrassed to tell anyone, although he recalls some of the other brothers had heard him muttering and shouting in his sleep most nights. I obviously enquired as to the nature of his dreams and nightmares; it was quite a shock I can tell you, professor."

The professor shifted in his chair and poured out some water from the jug on the desk.

"The brother explained to me how his dreams were antagonistic to his beliefs and that however hard he tried, he could not disregard certain regular unwanted images and words that came to him. The problem didn't improve and he would be missing for several days at a time; no-one knew where he was or had been."

"How long did this go on for?"

"Nearly a year, and then he disappeared at the end of September, just like Brother Gilbert."

"How many others have been affected?"

"Three more I'm aware of. What do you think is happening, professor?"

"Well, it sounds to me something similar to schizophrenia – but more than that."

"Do you believe in demonic possession, professor?"

"Frankly, no. But I have seen similar cases which I have no explanation for. Are your thoughts about possession based on your religious beliefs, abbot?"

"Only that it is a necessary fact: Because we believe in a benevolent God and angels, there also has to exist a malevolent Devil and demons. Those who give prayers for good and those who give curses for evil."

"I would agree with you, abbot, but then I'm afraid we'd both be wrong, because your logic is flawed, being based on a false premise."

"Well, I believe in what I trust to be true."

"Of course you do and so do I, but don't forget it was *you* who called *me* in to help with the problem and I'm a psychiatrist who deals with facts and truth based on evidence, not fiction and fantasy borne of delusion. You knew that."

"Touché, professor!"

"I would consider a mental disorder to be the likely cause – something driven by anxiety. Do you think that the affected brothers may be obsessively doubting their beliefs driven by their inner quest for truth and compulsively sabotaging them with blasphemy?"

"I really can't say, professor; I'll just have to leave that in your very capable hands and be available to help when I can."

"How many are affected at this moment?"

"Mercifully, only one – Brother Edward. He has become violent and evasive, especially when anyone tries to question him about it."

"Would *I* be able to speak with him?"

"I can only try to get him to come along and meet you, perhaps by using some other reason for you to see him and then you could see how far you can get in the interview," suggested the abbot.

"That's a good idea; I must give it some thought tonight."

"Brother Edward has entered that phase of going missing for a day or two. Last Wednesday and Thursday he didn't appear for prayers or for duties – he simply seemed to vanish like the others."

"Hopefully, I'll come up with something tomorrow."

He stood up and made for the study door, turning on his heel.

"May I explore the abbey grounds? I think it may help to inspire me."

"Of course, professor, feel free. Behind the abbey you will find the kitchen garden, cemetery and mausoleum where our brothers were interred during the centuries long ago. It's a bit desolate and windswept back there as it always has been - it's a part of the character of the place I suppose," he added.

Professor Benson thanked the abbot and went back to his room to reflect on his task ahead.

CHAPTER TWO

Walkabout

With only an hour before nightfall, the professor decided he would have a brief look around outside to familiarise himself with his surroundings. He found his way out through one of the back doors after mistakenly entering the kitchens where one of the brothers pointed the way.

The huge abbey was built on a piece of level ground and he wondered whether it had been levelled for the foundations all those centuries ago. Walking through the vegetable garden he passed on through a small gate onto the sparsely vegetated scrub-land and continued his uphill walk for about a hundred yards to where the cemetery was positioned. On through the cemetery gate he looked around at all the gravestones surrounding the central mausoleum.

The few inscriptions which were still legible after hundreds of years of erosion, revealed most of the interred were residents of Grimsfell dating back to the 1500s and only a few appeared to be the graves of monks; he guessed that the mausoleum must contain the others. He stopped to ponder whether the graves were cut into the underlying limestone, as the soil layer here would surely be too thin for a proper burial.

The mausoleum was long abandoned and neglected like the rest of the cemetery, with lumps of masonry missing, forming little piles of overgrown limestone debris. Ancient thick stems of ivy wove their way across and into the stonework probing the cracks, growing ever larger by the ever-green's increasing girth forcing the structure apart. Some of the stained glass of the arched windows still remained, but most had gone the way of the masonry, disappearing into the overgrown soil over years of neglect. However, the badly weathered doors were still intact and firmly shackled with rusted iron padlocks of considerable antiquity.

He could see that the building had a lower level by the long gaps every now and then along the lower edge of the side walls to allow some light and air to enter. He would very much like to see inside and made a mental note to ask the abbot for the keys.

The brooding mountain above seemed as threatening as it did protective, dwarfing the abbey and the small village further down towards the sea cliffs. Dusk was soon upon him as he turned to go back to the abbey gardens, when he glimpsed movement to the right of his field of vision. He saw a small group of large black birds approaching the abbey roof. That evening the abbot invited him to eat with them in the main hall.

"It's a bit dreary out the back in the winter; did you walk far?" enquired the abbot.

"Just as far as the mausoleum. It's quite a large building; does it go down far?"

"It seems to be on two levels, but I haven't been in there myself. It is said that at one time there was a well that reached down to the underground river and that the mausoleum was built next to it and later incorporated into the side of the building. It fell into disrepair centuries ago and as far as I'm aware no-one has ever explored it in recent times."

"Intriguing," commented the professor with eager thoughts of exploring it himself. "You have crows or ravens on the roof I saw last evening?"

"Yes, both, professor."

"Do they live in the roof of the abbey?"

"Apparently not. They just visit from time to time from elsewhere - just three ravens and a crow."

"A *crow*? Why are ravens with a crow?"

"Goodness knows!" replied the abbot, tucking in to his meal. "What are your plans for tomorrow with regard to Brother Edward?" he said, quickly changing the subject.

"I'm still thinking about it. Can you ask him if he would see me tomorrow afternoon?"

"Yes, I should see him at morning prayer. Do you plan to visit our little village down the hill?"

"Certainly. There are *two* places I would very much like to see whilst I'm here, abbot - the village and inside that mausoleum."

"I think the mausoleum is best left to its own devices, professor; it'll be far too dangerous to enter."

"Yes, I suppose that's right, but doesn't it fascinate you as to just what it looks like inside after all those centuries of neglect?"

"Well, yes it does, but there's little time to take on such an exploratory task as that, and the dangers of falling masonry would need to be evaluated carefully before anyone entered."

The professor's glass of wine went to his head and so he excused himself to bed.

The Halloween Chamber

The next morning he was up early and started making notes about how he should best interview Brother Edward to try and discover what was troubling him. As the weather was clement he decided he would take a walk down to the village before hopefully speaking with the troubled monk in the afternoon.

The walk from the abbey down to the village was very different from last evening's walk behind the abbey where he felt trapped between the huge abbey and the mountain. Ahead of him was the open sea with the village tucked inland about a quarter of a mile or so. A row of asymmetrical windswept trees bent by the insistent wind from the sea protected one another: the first in line being much smaller than the next because of the protection it provided by taking the full brunt of the wind, resulting in each tree being noticeably larger than the one before – he counted seven trees.

Passing the trees along the meandering pathway he came to the first cottage with its shutters firmly clamped to its windows and spotted a villager taking in her washing from the line between alarmingly leaning posts.

"Hello there!" he called, sounding of good cheer.

"Are you down from the abbey?" she asked, looking rather concerned.

"That's right; just sorting out a few problems for the abbot."

"Only there's something very strange going on up there."

"Really!"

"Well, some of the villagers go up there a couple of times a week to help with the cleaning and other things that need doing," she said, "but they come back with tales of weird behaviour by some of the monks."

"That's interesting, the abbot mentioned it too. What sort of weird behaviour?"

"We think it's some sort of madness. I'm not surprised, it would drive *me* mad being stuck up there all the time."

"Would I be able to speak with some of the people who work there?"

"I reckon the best place to ask would be at the pub – it's further along past the post office. You see that blue sign on the left?" She leant towards him and aimed a finger. "Well, that's the shop sign and the post office is next and then the pub – it's called The Witch's Brew."

"That sounds interesting – no bat's wings and spider's legs in the ale I hope!" he said with a chuckle.

"I wouldn't know, I rarely go in there," she replied drily, not appreciating his joke.

"Well, thanks for your help, I'll see what I can find out at the pub. What's your name by the way?"

"Rose . . . Rose Bennett," she hesitated.

"Thanks then, Rose, I'll be on my way." The professor turned giving a small wave to the attractive dark-haired young woman.

No-one else seemed to be around, so he reckoned they must all be in the pub. Just past the lonely looking red letterbox outside the post office, The Witch's Brew came into view, set back around a corner by one of the few trees in the village. Nailed to the tree was a tired-looking poster inviting people to the pub's Christmas celebrations next month entitled: *The Christmas Children*.

The pub was elaborately themed with all things witchy: what looked like a couple of stuffed black cats lurking in the shadows, lots of bats hanging precariously from the ceiling and the occasional old broomstick propped in the corners. As expected, it was low-beamed with an ancient-looking flag-stone floor, well worn into a shallow trough leading up to the bar. Small groups of people inhabited the dim alcoves around the single large room with a few of the locals appearing interested in the newcomer.

The professor spotted an old man sitting on his own leaning heavily on his robust knurled walking stick, looking exceptionally world-weary and asked him if he would like to join him for a drink.

"That's very kind of you sir," he said, touching his greasy hat. "I'll have the house ale, if you please."

"OK, I think I'll try it too."

The landlord finally emerged from the cellar clutching two bottles of red wine for a customer and set them down in front of a heavily bearded, long-haired man standing at the far end of the bar.

"There we are," he said triumphantly as he took the money from the man without a word of thanks in return, and turned to the professor. "What can I get for you?"

"I thought I would try the house ale, and one for the old gentleman too," he asked, turning to acknowledge him.

"Are you visiting these parts?" questioned the landlord looking him up and down suspiciously.

"I'm exploring really; I've just come down from the abbey," he explained. "Could you help me? I'm looking for anyone who works up there, just to ask them a few questions."

"*We've* got questions too," he said abruptly, lowering his eyebrows as if readying himself in anticipation of the details, exchanging glances with the old man.

"Is it about reports of the monks acting strangely?" asked the professor.

"You could say that; more like they're going mad. I've seen some of the monks wandering about near the cliffs and behind the old mausoleum over the years - couldn't make conversation though - it seemed like they were in a trance."

"That *is* interesting. I was contacted through my department at the university by the abbot to ask if I could investigate the cause of their disturbing and bizarre behaviour; my area of expertise really, although I'd be grateful if you could keep that to yourself."

"I could ask around to see if there's one of the cleaners who would speak to you. I'd like to know more too; you've got me intrigued now," he said, poking a finger into his straggly beard.

"If you wouldn't mind," the professor replied gratefully.

The old man listened intently but said nothing more as he savoured the house ale with one hand and held on firmly to his stick with the other.

"Well, I'll ask around. Can you call again tomorrow? Who shall I say is enquiring?"

"Professor Benson - I'm a doctor of psychiatry," he admitted, half expecting some sort of negative reaction from the landlord.

"A professor eh! I think you must be the only professor who's ever come to The Witch's Brew or even to all of Grimsfell! As I say, I'll ask around."

"Oh, by the way, what's the origin of the pub's name? Was this witch country at one time?"

"Legend has it that an old crone, name of Alice Bennett, once lived here in the village and had preyed on young women and children. If you're interested I'll tell you more about it when I see you tomorrow."

"That's kind of you – if it's no bother. My profession is trying to understand the mind, so it's quite relevant to try and understand what turns people's minds to the supernatural belief in gods, demons and witches. I'll see you tomorrow."

The old man looked up and touched his hat.

There was still time to do a bit more exploring before dusk, so the professor walked behind the pub and followed a little path back in the direction of the cliffs along by a cemetery and a series of vegetable garden allotments which had seen better days. A rugged looking woman struggling with an enormous wheelbarrow appeared from behind a ramshackle shed. The professor called out to her:

"Do you need a hand with that, my dear?"

"No, I'll be fine, nearly there, thanks."

"I thought I'd go down to the sea. Which is the best way?"

"Go along the path towards that hill," she pointed. "That's The Lovers' Way to the cliff crag above the sea where all the courting goes on. From there you'll see a steep path down to the sea. Mind you, there're no beaches here – just wee rocky bays you can only get to by their own paths. You'll need sturdy boots for those, so as not to lose your footing; it really is treacherous so you take care."

"Well thanks for the warning - I'll see how I get on."

After following the pathway for a while, the professor reached the small hill and trudged to the top of the cliffs. Ahead, and down an incline, he could see a large chunk of rock jutting out above the sea. More of a Lovers' Leap he thought. Further along the path he could see the way down to a tiny rock-strewn beach far below. Not for him he thought, turning his direction and then his thoughts to the afternoon's meeting.

Exhausted after his walk back up to the abbey, he lay down on his bed with his notes in his hand to finalise how he would conduct the interview, that is if the abbot was able to get the monk's agreement.

At lunch the abbot confirmed that Brother Edward was willing to be interviewed and that he had told him he didn't really know what it was about, other than an interview about life as a resident at the abbey for some research project for a visiting Professor Benson. The professor thought that was a clever idea and started to rewrite some of his notes.

The little monk he had met when he first arrived brought him a message from the abbot to say the interview was planned for an hour's time and was that all right. Confirming this, the professor sat on his bed in a dilemma – which colour bow tie would best suit the situation? He was well aware of the psychological effects of this coloured point of focus which had been the subject of many afternoon tea debates at the university.

Wearing a bright red bow tie, the professor knocked on the abbot's study door. Abbot Gregory opened the door and appeared with a concerned expression upon his face as he beckoned for him to come inside.

"He's rather agitated," he whispered.

The professor nodded as he moved over to where Brother Edward was sitting with his back to the door while the abbot left the room.

"Hello, I'm Professor Benson, and I'm very grateful for your time. I wanted to know about aspects of monastic life through your experience for part of a research paper I plan to write. It's a life which very few people are familiar with and so it will be interesting to compare and contrast to normal life," explained the professor, convincingly he thought. The man slowly raised his head and nodded. He looked terrible, as if he hadn't slept for a week.

"What would you like to know?"

"About what you do here and how the day goes for you, and how you get on with the other brothers - general things really. Do you want to continue, because you don't look too well?" he felt compelled to ask.

"I'm going crazy."

"*Crazy?*" he asked in a deliberately concerned voice.

"I don't know what I'm doing half the time. My mind feels controlled and I have these bad thoughts."

"Do you want to talk about that instead – off the record?"

"I *do* need help . . . *Please,*" he anguished.

The professor sat down beside him.

"How can I help?" he said softly.

"I have to do things I don't want to do."

"*Who* is making you do things?"

"That's the problem, I don't know . . . it's just that I'm compelled by thoughts and images that insist I must do them . . . thinking things I don't want to think . . . preparing me for something."

"The abbot tells me you went away for a few days; where did you go?"

"But *that* was a dream . . . *wasn't* it?"

"Brother Edward, *when* did you start to feel unwell and controlled?"

"Around two years ago I began to have bad dreams and then nightmares. What are dreams and what's reality is blurred, and it became worse over the last year or so. Horrible visions torment me and convince me to leave the abbey and steal a child from the village. I know I must do this soon and I practiced it in a dream . . . but you say it *wasn't* a dream and that I'd gone missing for a few days?"

"That's what the abbot told me, and your brothers would have known, but probably didn't like to say. I don't know."

The Halloween Chamber

"My head is screaming - aching - because I want to tell you about the details and images in my dreams and nightmares . . . but I just daren't reveal them to anyone."

"Why not? . . . What will happen if you tell me?" said the professor kindly.

"*Terrible* things; that's all I dare say. I'm sorry but I'm not myself."

"That's fine brother, you *must* rest now, and if you wish to speak further about this please feel free to call on me any time because we must try and understand this disturbing mystery and get you well again."

"Thank you professor. I'm sorry we didn't get to talk about life at the abbey in the sense you wanted for your research. I haven't a life at the moment . . . it's been drained out of me."

Professor Benson helped Brother Edward from his chair and called for another brother to help take him to his room and then returned to his own room to make notes before supper.

The Halloween Chamber

CHAPTER THREE

The Grimsfell Witch

The professor had trouble sleeping that night with so many questions on his mind which he wanted answering. After breakfast he was taken aside by abbot Gregory.

"Professor, it's happened again – Brother Edward has gone missing. Do you think we should just wait to see if he returns or should we go and look for him? We can gather up a little search party later on."

"I guess it's best we look for him in case he's injured. Do you know if the brothers frequent the cliffs?"

"Why do you ask?"

"Because a chap in the village said he'd sometimes seen monks from the abbey walking near the sea – and the mausoleum," he added.

"I'm sure that's possible - overlooking the sea from up high is a good place to sit and think."

"It's dangerous up there."

"Quite so professor. I've also occasionally seen brothers venture beyond the vegetable garden and up to the cemetery - to look at the names on the stones I would imagine. As I've said, our mausoleum has long been closed and derelict, and I'm sure no-one goes there."

"I'm going down to the village again this morning, so shall we all meet up after lunch to have a look around? I'll keep my eyes open in the village."

"Yes, I'll see if any of the brothers can spare an hour or two from their duties; I'm sure they are as concerned as we are."

After leaving the abbey by the front gates, the professor walked around the back and looked up towards the mausoleum at the base of the mountain. He couldn't help thinking that the building was holding a sinister secret and must be investigated.

Back at The Witch's Brew he sat down at one of the trestle tables in the central area of the room. A few people were in the alcoves, but nowhere near as many as yesterday. The landlord bustled in the door laden with bread and vegetables in woven wicker baskets and acknowledged the professor on his way to the kitchen; he soon joined him at the table.

"Well, that's most of today's meals sorted out - just need to collect the eggs and chickens from the farm. Do you still want to hear the story of Alice Bennett?"

"Wait a minute! Alice Bennett did you say - the witch? Because I met a *Rose* Bennett yesterday."

"Rose says she is a descendant of the centuries-old Bennett family who lived in the village when it was much smaller. The story goes that Alice had three brothers who became monks at the abbey while she stayed at home with her father; her mother had died when her youngest brother was born. Alice took long walks up to the crag - Lovers' Crag as it's now called - and was often seen staring out to sea. The Bennett women would never marry, so as to keep their name.

"The next part of the story describes how she disappeared for many days at a time, but no-one knew where she'd gone or saw her leave. It's all here in these old papers which were found in the wall when we put in the extra window there by the stairs," he pointed.

He clutched the papers in one hand and his ale in the other and continued:

"The young folk used the crag for somewhere out of the way for their courting - they still do - but the young women began to change personality and seemed to age prematurely, eventually becoming withered, stooping crones. The young men turned away from them and soon afterwards these women vanished."

The landlord was leaning forward, rather enjoying telling the story that gave his pub its name and the professor wondered if he was just making it all up. He continued his story:

"The parents and friends searched everywhere for their daughters, but could find no clue as to the reason for their disappearance. That's when folk started putting two and two together: Alice Bennett was missing at the same times as the women," he added excitedly gathering up saliva. "Then, in the thirties, the cave was discovered by a group of young fossil hunters."

"A *cave*?"

"Beneath the crag they found a cave, but not just any old crack in the cliff mind you! No. It ties up with what's described in the old papers - this cave was home to a witch's coven. Alice Bennett was one of the witches who was able to use magic spells to influence the young girls meeting their lovers on the crag immediately above the cave entrance. They regularly chanted and gesticulated to gradually sap the passion and lust from them until they eventually became ugly crones. It was the magical energy by which they were able to procure more of their kind, by eventually luring them into their secret coven within the cave.

"Centuries ago, so the story goes, the villagers got into the cave and set about attacking and murdering the witches - all except Alice who miraculously changed into an immortal crow and flew out of the cave to safety."

The landlord looked up at the professor to see his reaction to the climax of his tale. "Damn! You couldn't make it up could you?"

"*Well*, that's exactly what I need to ask you: *Did* you make it up to create interest in visiting the pub together with the witch's theme?"

The landlord looked shocked and crestfallen at the professor's suggestion and stared back at him with convincing eyes. "I tell you, it's all here!" he said shaking the tattered papers and offering them to be looked at. The professor took them from him and made a space on the large table to lay them out – one by one.

"They certainly *look* old, but not *that* old! Perhaps someone thought it up and hid the papers in the wall as a joke a long time ago, just for someone like yourself to believe it."

"But that part of the wall we removed was the original from when it was built – I'm sure of that. It used to be a large farmhouse with an adjoining barn, built centuries ago."

"Who, exactly, is telling these stories?" queried the professor.

"They're stories handed down from generation to generation – you know, and these papers seem to confirm it."

"I *do* know that stories change a bit every time they're retold, perhaps with fanciful additions to make it more interesting and exciting – something that people like to believe – like flying saucers. A couple of years after the war ended a disc was described as having crashed on a farm in the US, and from then on it was visitors from space - everyone and his dog were seeing them."

"But the disappearances . . . they're still going on from the abbey *and* children from the village . . . it could all be linked, professor."

"I doubt it. It's still in the realms of supernatural fiction with the abbot telling me that the monks seem to be possessed by demons up until they vanish. It's very similar I'll grant you that. Does Rose know about this?"

"I think she does, but doesn't like to dwell on thoughts that her great-great-great relative, however many 'greats' it is, was a witch, however unbelievable and bizarre."

An hour had past and the professor thanked the landlord for the story and asked if he would keep the papers safe for him to examine at a later time.

On arriving back at the abbey, the search party was organised and gathering at the front of the building headed by the abbot, resplendent in a green waxed jacket and matching green Wellington boots and gloves.

"I'm sorry I'm a bit late," called out the professor. "Heard a good story at the pub."

It was decided to check around the cliffs, arming various monks with binoculars to scan the little coves. The abbot had mustered about a dozen brothers who trekked in a long line down to the cliffs and up the little hill to the perilous rocky cliff edge.

Two hours later they were none the wiser; no evidence of Brother Edward was found. Professor Benson made the bold suggestion that it would be a good idea to look inside the mausoleum.

"No, it's been shut up for centuries as far as I know," piped up a brother at the back of the group. "It would be too risky for us to go in there."

The professor's suspicions were immediately raised: Did this fellow know something he didn't want the rest of them to find out about? The abbot shook his head and decided it was too near dusk for anyone to venture into the dangerous old building with just torches.

"Some of us will have a look there tomorrow he suggested. Now for some supper."

That evening the professor retold the witch story to abbot Gregory who seemed to listen intently.

"Well. What do you think? See any links?"

"A crow you say - immortal? This Alice Bennett became a *crow* and flew away to safety in the story," commented the abbot.

"Yes, a *crow*."

"The other day you said you saw ravens *and a crow* flying up to the abbey roof?"

"Coincidence. Just coincidence. Are you saying we are dealing with the supernatural here?"

"It's just a possibility, for I too have a story to tell that's been passed on here at the abbey for centuries, not just by word of mouth either – it's been written as fact and updated centuries ago in a book in the library. In light of what you've told me, it may be relevant, otherwise I wouldn't have mentioned it."

"Can I see the book?" asked the professor eagerly.

"Yes, we can go along and you can read it for yourself, if you would rather that than me tell you from memory."

"I would like to see it anyway if you have the time."

The Halloween Chamber

The vast library was in the ancient Gothic part of the abbey which, along with the crypt, had miraculously survived a terrible fire centuries before. Tall, narrow windows illuminated by day and electric light when needed. The abbot flicked a long row of brown Bakelite switches and lamps lit up along the tops of the shelves. At the far end of the library stood a large, sturdy wooden cabinet which protected some of the more valuable and rare volumes. He produced an old set of keys on a rusting ring and selected the appropriate key and slipped it into the lock. The brass-framed glass door was held open by an ornate levered arrangement, also of brass.

"Here it is!" exclaimed the abbot as he reached in to retrieve the gilt-edged book. "Smaller than I remember."

Some pages fell open easily whilst others stubbornly stuck together, but with careful manipulation the abbot allowed them to reveal their contents.

"The first mention is here in the sixteenth century: 1539, if I can read it – my translation's a bit rusty these days – not much call for it. It says that some monks had left their duties and could not be found. Also, that they were blasphemous and displayed rudeness to their fellow brothers with no explanation. A later entry tells of the discovery of a secret chamber next to the abbey crypt where '*the monks were seen and heard to blaspheme openly with gesticulation not of their training. Conjuring demonic forms to their satisfaction resulting in ecstatic posturing*'.

"Another entry here, much later in 1564, refers to the same practise which had to be ended by force. It tells of the underground river which served our wells and whose provenance is from beneath Oros – that's our mountain. The force needed to overcome the demonic brothers led to them throwing themselves into the river and were '*swept violently away'* it says, but with the exception of three monks who were sibling brothers who *'held themselves together with the force of many demons and escaped through the air above the river as ravens'*. Professor, dare I say it? You saw three ravens and a crow. But here's the link: the three brothers' surname was Bennett."

"My goodness! This *is* interesting. So we have four siblings, the Bennetts, who were supposedly born in the village: three males who become demonic monks here in this abbey in the sixteenth century and their sister who becomes a witch during the same period - all with the power to transform themselves into corvids - three male ravens and a female crow - to live forever."

"It's difficult to believe, professor, but it looks as if they are still active here - immortal no less." By now the abbot was sitting down, trying to take in fiction which appeared to be fact.

Witches Bring Children to the Devil - Woodcut 1591

COVEN

Underneath the rocky crags,
Lived a coven of old hags.
Beware their evil magic spell,
It will send you straight to Hell.

Tongue of bat and foot of crow,
What they'll do is hard to know.
As the cauldron starts to boil,
Someone's life is set to spoil.

Lovers walk the crags above,
Sending out the power of love.
This the witches drain away,
For their spells the lovers pay.

At end of day the sunlight fades,
No longer falling on the glades.
Now is heard the dreadful drone,
Of each and every wretched crone.

The Halloween Chamber

CHAPTER FOUR

Mausoleum

Neither the professor nor the abbot slept much that night and both met up rather late during breakfast. Abbot Gregory spoke first:

"Did you eventually get off to sleep only to awaken thinking last night's revelation was a dream, professor?"

"I do wish it was only that, but I'm rather concerned to say the least, as to what we will find in the mausoleum. I meant to ask you about this underground river - have you seen it?"

"Not seen it, just heard of it from that book. There's nothing about a secret chamber or a river entrance *I* know of near the crypt, but I suppose it may well have been walled-up after the death of the monks. Certainly worth investigating."

"*After* we've looked in the mausoleum."

"Not looking forward to that one, but we *must* try to find Brother Edward, I'm guessing he *might* be in there. Shall we start at ten?"

"Yes, if I can summon up the courage," the professor winced.

"I'll sort out the torches and we'll just have to see how far we get. We'll do this without the others being involved."

"Certainly," replied the professor, "just in case things go horribly wrong."

The Oros mountain seemed more menacing than usual as it towered protectively over the cemetery building. On this dull day they arrived at the mausoleum doors.

"So, there are no keys to these padlocks? They're rust-welded anyway, we'll have to force them open. Did you pack the crowbar?"

"I have it here. Shall we take turns?" said the abbot with a wry smile.

"OK, *you* start - it's your mausoleum," cracked the professor.

The emergence of humour at this point momentarily took their mind off the task, but neither could guess what lay ahead.

Groaning, creaking, flaking iron finally gave way to the prying crowbar as the hasps ruptured, but the ancient robust doors remained firmly wedged shut after centuries of damp and decay. The professor took up the crowbar and thrust its nail-pulling end into the crumbling wood beneath one door's hinges until they finally succumbed to his determined efforts and the door was able to be heaved open enough for them to squeeze through. Sheets of dusty cobwebs drifted menacingly down over their heads as they fought their way through to stand inside the structure at last. As their eyes accommodated to the dingy, dusty dimness, rows of Gothic arches could be seen stretching either side the length of the building. Between the rows ran an enclosing balustrade, separating the ground floor from a wide stone stairway descending into ominous blackness.

"We'll shine both torches into each of the arched recesses if we're going to do this methodically," the professor decided.

Each alcove contained a burial casket, some of wood and others of stone, positioned against the far wall. Centuries of dust and debris strewn across the floor revealed small animal skeletons of rats, bats and birds, their small dismantled bodies laid to rest in a place built for the purpose.

"Well, that's the first row checked - no Brother Edward here." stated the professor unreverentially. "Now for the other side."

Abbot Gregory found himself following the rather more eager professor on his quest to reveal the secrets of the mausoleum. Having thoroughly checked the ground floor alcoves they each shone their torch down the deep stone stairway.

"After you abbot!" he joked, more in fear than humour.

It was no easy matter negotiating each step, as each was littered with the same debris as everywhere else and had to be kicked aside to secure sure footing before the next step. Torchlight lit the stairway walls and the immediate steps, but could not show what lay below. Finally, the last step revealed itself as they hit level ground.

"It seems to be just a repeat of upstairs," remarked the professor. "More archways and more alcoves." He spotted a large, iron-banded wooden chest positioned at the side of the casket in one of the alcoves, but that would have to wait until another day.

The heavy, fusty air was difficult to breath as they continued their careful search for evidence of Brother Edward, in fact for evidence of any of the vanished monks.

The building was evidently just on two levels as expected, but they hadn't seen the well which was reportedly incorporated within the lower level. Shining his torch around one last time the professor noticed a flagstone partially misplaced in the floor, as if someone had tried to lift it and not replaced it properly.

"Perhaps that's the well," the professor whispered.

"Why are you whispering?" commented the abbot in another fear-induced episode of humour.

The crowbar was again put to work to move the slab aside. Inch by inch the ever increasing gap allowed an evil stench to pervade their nostrils, and then they heard a sound – the sound of rushing water. The abbot caught his breath to speak.

"That's the river then, and something's rotting down there!" They both gave each other a prolonged stony stare, fearing the worst. Once removed, the slab revealed narrow stone steps inviting the pair to investigate the unknown depths of the mausoleum.

"*You're* going first this time, professor."

"I *knew* you were going to say that!"

Wedging the crowbar over the corner of the opening provided a handhold as the professor carefully lowered himself down, all the time fighting against retching. They couldn't stay in this place for long.

At the bottom of twelve stone steps the professor's torch light opened up a good-sized stone room hewn into the limestone with an arched exit to a river tunnel on the far side opposite the steps entrance arch. Investigation of the remaining four sides of the hexagonal chamber revealed concave, backward-sloping, arch-topped alcoved walls set at an angle of about seventy degrees to a hexagonal floor, and the floor itself incorporating a carved, round basin about fifteen feet across with a raised aperture in the middle; above their heads a central opening in the vaulted roof.

The Halloween Chamber

"What's this all about!?" exclaimed the professor in surprise. "There are triangular markings, engravings in the centre of each of the alcove walls - come and see what you think."

Each curved alcove wall had a large, deeply inscribed inverted pentagram upon it, with the two pairs of alcoves opposite one another. Turning his torch towards the professor, the abbot illuminated the entrance to the river tunnel, revealing the eyeless, rotting, mutilated corpse of Brother Edward.

"I'm getting out of here!" the abbot shouted and clambered the cold stone steps on his hands and knees in his haste, with the professor right behind him.

The crowbar dislodged, ringing and clattering its way down the stone steps to the chamber floor below, audibly adding to the fearful tension and anxiety felt by the intrepid explorers. The pair explosively dislodged the debris cluttering the floors and steps as they made their way up to the shaft of light at the place they had entered the mausoleum more than two hours earlier.

It was impossible for them to keep secret what they had found as they returned to the abbey through the kitchen garden, alarming the brothers preparing the mid-day meal. Panic was written all over their faces and questions flowed fast and furious as to what had happened to Brother Edward.

The abbey residents were in shock as gradually over the next few hours their story was told about the discovery of their fellow brother. But it was decided on the way back not to mention the pentagram symbols in the weird, hexagonal stone chamber; there was already enough bad news to take in.

The Halloween Chamber

The professor decided that his evening would be best spent trying to relax in his room listening to music on the Pye radio provided in the corner of his room; he had to unwind to clear his mind enough to plan what he should do next. He was about to retire to bed when there was a soft knock on his door.

"Hello! Who's there?" he called. There was no reply so he partially opened the door and was surprised to see the monk who had welcomed him on his arrival.

"I didn't call out it was me for fear of being caught."

"Caught for what? What have you done?"

"I need to speak with you now that I know what happened to Brother Edward. You see your life's in danger now you've discovered The Halloween Chamber and so will mine be if I'm caught speaking to you."

"Go on."

"Another of the brothers, Brother Thomas, is troubled and confided in me. He told me that satanic forces are being summoned to exact revenge on the people of Grimsfell and the abbey and that he was chosen to do the work Brother Edward had refused to undertake, and that's why they killed him."

"Who is *they*? I'm sorry, what is your name?"

"Brother Dawson; I came here ten years ago."

"Can you arrange for me to meet Brother Thomas, perhaps in the grounds this evening?"

"He doesn't know I'm telling you and *he's* the one who's being prepared to kill you."

"Who *or what* is preparing him to kill me?"

"The miasma . . . from the river tunnel. Brother Thomas told me the river runs underground from the mountain, under the mausoleum and then under the abbey and out to the sea - underwater. Another passage leads up into a cave inside the cliffs – the one they say was used by a witch's coven. The miasma is produced in the The Halloween Chamber by the three immortal ravens and a crow. They fly into the witch's cave and up along the river tunnel to the Chamber where they transform back into the Bennett siblings' human form. Their satanic rituals bring forth the demon who disintegrates into the evil, mind-altering miasma in such quantity that the vapour fills the river tunnel and then flows downhill above the water to beneath the abbey and insidiously pervades the building. It is capable of turning the minds of susceptible people to do the will of its creator: the demon summoned by the Bennetts in retribution for Grimsfell folk forcing them to exist as corvids evermore.

"On one day a year, All Hallows' Eve, October the thirty-first, when the membrane between the good overworld and the evil underworld is at its most fragile, the power of evil can break through and wreak havoc on the living. The Halloween Chamber acts as a portal between these worlds."

"If all this is true, why are you risking your life telling me?"

"Because Brother Edward was my dear friend. I had to watch him succumb to the evil power of the miasma. Brother Thomas and both Brother Edward and I, are caring susceptible people and I may be the next in line to suffer from its evil influence. It is now November, but the miasma is so clinging that it remains beneath the abbey for many weeks, continually permeating the building."

"But how was Brother Edward killed?"

"Brother Thomas didn't say. That's when I decided to tell you about it; you may be able to find a way - perhaps through science. He cannot prevent attempting to kill you because you are a threat to the determined intentions of the Bennetts to cause suffering to all here in Grimsfell for what happened nearly four centuries ago."

Long after Brother Dawson left, the professor endured a restless night, his mind awash with trying to decide what to do, and if he really *was* in danger from this deranged monk.

The next day two police cars and a van arrived outside the abbey gates, responding to the abbot's report that a body had been found. Officers gathered the monks into small groups to get a general idea of circumstances leading up to Brother Edward's disappearance. Meanwhile, the mausoleum doors were being wrenched open wide to remove the body from the subterranean chamber. The question arose as to how the body came to be where it was found, because the only open access to the chamber at the time was by the river tunnel.

Policemen in waders passed down the stone steps of The Halloween Chamber and on through the opening into the tunnel. Although fast flowing, it was shallow and rocky and perfectly possible to navigate. One hundred yards downstream they found themselves next to a ledge with stone steps leading up into the depths of the abbey foundations next to the crypt and into an elaborately carved large room set out with a central black granite altar with satanic inscriptions over the cobweb festooned walls and ceiling. It was difficult to see, despite their torches, but eventually the team of investigators discovered a sealed-up entrance way at the opposite end of the chamber to the river tunnel entrance that was found to lead directly into the abbey crypt, the way Brother Edward was taken.

The doctor who had examined the body before its removal walked over from his car towards the abbot.

"He was in a right old mess, I can tell you – not much of his face left. I gather you saw that when you found him in that hell-hole?"

"To tell you the truth, I didn't stay to look. Do you know how he died?"

"I do. But you're not going to believe it," said the doctor with a fixed intent stare. "He was *pecked* to death. We found black feathers that must have dislodged during the attack."

The abbot recoiled in horror, his mind still fresh with images of ravens and crows from the recent revelations. He quickly composed himself, not wanting to reveal the relevant content of the supernatural stories of corvids. He had to think quickly.

"Perhaps it was the abbey raven's territory and they attacked him to protect it," he concluded.

"Do you have many ravens at the abbey?" asked the doctor.

"I've seen a few flying around the roof," he hastily added.

"Well, it's most unusual; I've heard of seagulls attacking for a few chips, but not murderous subterranean ravens."

The whole day was taken up with police activity and the crypt's hidden entrance slab was replaced after photographs of the satanic room were taken. It was a welcome peace that settled on Grimsfell abbey that evening as the professor decided to take the evening air.

*   *   *

The following day one of the brothers passed on a message to the professor that had been received from the landlord of The Witch's Brew, asking him to come down to the village because he had some more information for him.

It was a fine but chilly walk down to the village pub.

"I'm glad you could call," said the landlord. "I hadn't told you my name . . . it's George Morgan," he revealed.

"I'll have some of that fine witch's brew of yours then George - and have one yourself."

"There's things I hadn't told you about the missing children," he began. "Every so often, over the years, children disappear and are never found. They are always descendants of the ancient village people . . . never newcomer's children."

"What do the police make of it then, George?"

"They're as puzzled as we are that it always occurs at Christmas time - we've come to call them the Christmas Children. It's all very sad. Of course, some folk here think it's all to do with Alice seeking revenge from the past. I wondered whether you'd find it a useful addition to your investigation?"

"When did the last child vanish from the village, George?"

"Nearly three years ago, a seven year old girl name of Florence Fleming was last seen feeding a neighbour's chickens on a December morning in nineteen fifty. The devastated parents, the police and the villagers' searches came to nothing . . . it went on for weeks." His words started to crack and he gave a cough.

"I'm so sorry to hear this; we *must* get to the truth of this grisly mystery. Can it possibly be true that ancient deranged monks and a witch are responsible? Common sense tells me it can't be, but something strange *is* going on which would be described as paranormal . . . and it's *that* time of year again."

CHAPTER FIVE

Escape

Professor Benson went on his now regular late afternoon walk - it helped him to think. Dusk fell over Grimsfell as he looked out over the hillside and cliffs towards the sea with a November chill in the air. The wind had dropped and the stillness felt quite surreal with only the sound of the distant waves upon the rocks far below and the moonlight creating an intense eerie light.

On his way back he noticed a brother was standing by one of the straggly cypress trees with his hood up against the cold.

"Got a bit much in there today; are you enjoying the fresh night air too?" the professor called out as he approached.

"I wanted to speak with you if that's all right?" said the monk quietly.

"Certainly. Did you want to go back inside or shall we talk here?"

"We'll talk here," said the brother insistently, walking behind a tree by the abbey wall, furtively peering out from under his hood.

The professor followed, eager to hear what he had to say.

"You know too much."

"What did you say?"

"I must eliminate you," he said, pulling his hood to one side to reveal a hideous facial contortion as if he was fighting against what he had just said. "I'm sorry, I can't help myself – it's too strong."

"Steady on! *What's* too strong? Perhaps we'd better go inside."

"I have to protect my masters. I have to kill you," he whispered as he put his arm around the professor's shoulders.

"I guess you are Brother Thomas?"

"How do you know that?" he said angrily with his voice now raised.

"It's my job to know these things," he explained lamely, deciding what to do next.

Suddenly, Brother Thomas lunged at him with a knife. The professor moved at the last split second and the weapon stuck into his shoulder as he instinctively punched out at his assailant. Above them appeared the ravens as if from nowhere, swirling and diving at the professor with their huge beaks tearing at his face. He ran along by the wall and out behind the abbey to the cemetery and beyond the mausoleum, fighting off the birds trying to tear his head to pieces.

Soon, he was at the foot of Oros, still running and looking for cover in the half-light, wiping away the blood streaming from his shoulder and face, all the while grateful at least that Brother Thomas had missed his heart and was now nowhere to be seen. He had no idea where he was, but carried on running all the same, lashing out at the flying black enemy whenever he could, landing some satisfying punches. After a while he was sure the ravens had either lost him or given up the chase for now, but thought it prudent to wedge himself into one of the many large rock fissures.

He was no longer a young man and fought the exhaustion as best he could, wiping the blood from his eyes and jamming his wound with his handkerchief as he drifted into dreams.

"Do you need some help?" A voice penetrated his mind, but the professor was only dreaming. "Here let me look at that wound. What happened?" the voice said with an educated accent.

Dragging himself half awake he became aware of the glare of a torch and a scruffy man standing next to him – helping him in his hour of need.

"Stabbed! I was bloody stabbed by one of the monks at the abbey. Where did you come from?"

"I live here . . . on, or rather *in*, the mountain," he said matter-of-factly.

The professor conveyed his gratitude to the mountain man who wrapped his shoulder with his scarf and began mopping his face with his handkerchief whilst explaining how he had become a hermit:

"I was a monk at the abbey many years ago and had to escape with my life because of the evil things that went on there, and I never went back. I like it here on the mountain, well away from any trouble and close to nature. Not too good in the winter mind you, but I have a wonderful big house. I call it a house, but really it's an enormous cave. There's an extensive cave system running throughout this side of the mountain," he explained enthusiastically.

As the professor gradually regained his strength and composure on the cold, bleak mountainside, he told the comforting stranger who he was and why he was at the abbey and also what had been discovered beneath the mausoleum.

The Halloween Chamber

"You've found The Halloween Chamber and the Oros river tunnel then?"

"How did *you* discover it all?" asked the professor.

"I simply followed the tunnel downhill from beneath my cave by torchlight, many years ago now. I've seen what goes on at Halloween under the old mausoleum - it's horrific. I've been just outside the Chamber's river entrance and witnessed the evil for myself; I only ever did that once more.

"I've seen the four black birds fly up through the tunnel, from the Witch's Cave I guess, as that's open to the outside on the cliff. They position themselves on the four walls of the Chamber at mid-day on Halloween and transform back to their human form as the Bennett siblings. They chant away in some demon language to procure the presence of what I can only describe as an evil entity that's half corporeal and half gas. It emanates from the orifice in the floor like an evil fart from the Devil himself - the Devil's arse-hole I call it."

"Brother Dawson told me this too, but how could you see all this happening without them spotting you?"

"They are too far gone in their frenzied work to notice the torchlight, besides, there's some daylight from the open well shaft above, through the centre of the ceiling. The next phase is even more disturbing: the gaseous demon changes into a thick miasma to become millions of separate entities - I call them *miasmids*. They flow copiously out the river entrance and down to beneath the abbey. That's the evil which permeates the abbey to turn good monks like me into automaton *evilids* to do the bidding of the evil collective mind-force of the Bennetts."

"You escaped from the abbey? Sorry, I hadn't asked your name."

"I'm Duncan. I escaped much the same as you. In a more

lucid moment after I'd become affected, I ran from the abbey to here - Oros, and discovered the caves; I've lived here ever since. Come inside and see."

Duncan helped the ailing professor to his feet and led him higher up the slope. Removing an old wooden fence behind a scraggy bush revealed an opening into the vast limestone wall.

"How did you find the entrance?"

"Luck . . . pure luck - you need some occasionally," he said philosophically. "But this isn't the *only* way into the system - I've found many more over the years."

"Well, I was certainly lucky that you found me when you did - I could easily have bled to death," said the professor, warmly shaking Duncan's hand with his good arm.

The narrow limestone entrance-way became gradually larger and then suddenly opened up into a large high-ceilinged chamber.

"Just along here is my living room," he smiled.

"That's good!" sighed the relieved professor hanging off of Duncan's shoulder, "I could do with a nice long sit down."

Much to his surprise, Duncan's living room *did* have what appeared in the flash of torchlight, to be a dilapidated settee.

"Put it together myself . . . after I'd sawn it into three pieces to get it through the rock," he explained proudly. "Someone in the next village had left it out for the dustbin men, so I made good use of it," he said, plonking himself down, accompanied by a cacophony of creaks. "I also have some old cupboards and boxes - lots and lots of boxes. Excuse me for a moment." Duncan lit an enormous oil lamp before going to another part of the cave and came back with bandages, a cloth and a bottle of yellow fluid.

"I keep these for emergencies."

"Have you got a kitchen sink too?" asked the professor, nervously joking.

"I have a large sturdy pail," he said proudly. "I light a fire in the corner for cooking and when it's really cold, but the smoke's a problem when it blows back in if it's too windy out there. I'd discovered there's a natural updraught in here through an opening at the very top where the smoke tends to be drawn to, but I haven't explored where it comes out - it's inaccessibly steep outside. The temperature stays pretty constant in caves, so it's quite pleasant."

"I have to return to the abbey soon, Duncan," said the professor resolutely, "even though my life's in danger. I have a plan to end this madness if you could help me; it will be too difficult and dangerous for me to do alone. But, essentially, we could ambush the Halloween ritual by creeping down the river tunnel on the morning of the thirty-first next year. If we can attack and kill the Bennett siblings in human form they will no longer be immortal as corvids to continue repeating their yearly evil."

"Sounds feasible. I just need you to convince me that you're not raving mad. OK, how much do you know about Grimsfell village?"

"I'll tell you what I know, Duncan: It's where the Bennetts came from centuries ago, and that Alice, the witch, is thought to be partly responsible for turning young women into witches for her coven and abducting children, according to papers uncovered by the landlord of The Witch's Brew pub," explained the professor. "Her revenge for having spent centuries as a crow, is to meet with her raven brothers each Halloween to conjure the miasmic demon from the portal between the worlds of good and evil. Also, that often around Christmas time, a village child goes missing, never to be seen or heard of again. George, the landlord told me this, he seemed keen for me to know.

"It seems the demonic monks, transformed by the miasma, are driven to wander around the village during the following month or two, intent on kidnapping a child just before Christmas as Bennett revenge-puppets against the murderous actions the villagers and monks took centuries before."

"Sounds crazy doesn't it, but that's the truth of the matter, prof."

After much more discussion, Duncan agrees to the plan and three weeks later the professor feels well enough to attempt his return to the abbey.

The Halloween Chamber

CHAPTER SIX

The Miasmic Demon

The professor's wounds had healed well under Duncan's care and he readies himself for his journey back to the abbey.

"I don't know my way, Duncan, could you point me in the right direction in the morning?"

"Sure, but how are you going to explain your scars to the abbot?"

"I'll tell him exactly what happened and hope that Brother Thomas doesn't have another go at me."

"Will you contact the police?"

"I think it'll make things too complicated if I do. I'll check the lie of the land before I decide on further plans."

The next morning the professor followed Duncan out of his limestone living room and out on to the mountainside. Everywhere looked the same to the professor as he picked his way over the rocks and tough clumps of grass. Around a quarter of a mile or so the abbey became visible in the distance below them.

"I don't know how long I'll stay at the abbey, Duncan. How shall we make contact?"

The Halloween Chamber

"My good friend Brother Dawson knows where I am and you can trust him. If anything new turns up just let him know and he'll find me," explained Duncan. "Will you be able to return next October for us to execute your plan?"

"We'll definitely meet up to decide the details, Duncan. Thanks again."

The professor continued his way down past the mausoleum and the cemetery to the kitchen garden and entered through the kitchen door, keen to find the abbot to explain the situation.

That day's kitchen staff were surprised to see him looking the worse for wear and offered him food and drink.

"I got lost on the mountain," he explained, "after tumbling down a steep slope. I eventually made it to the next village and some kind ladies took me in and patched me up. I've only just recovered enough to return." He didn't want the truth to be known about their murderous brother. "Is the abbot around?"

"He came to morning prayer and he usually returns to his room for the day's paperwork," said one.

"OK, thanks. I'll see if I can hunt him down."

He decides to go to his old room for a change of clothes, hoping it was still as he had left it. After a welcome wash and rest he went down to the abbot's study.

"Goodness gracious me! Where *have* you been, professor?" exclaimed the startled abbot.

"My late afternoon walk the other week turned out to be a bit too adventurous. I was attacked by Brother Thomas and three ravens."

He continued to explain the details of that evening and his meeting with the hermit monk, whom the abbot knew as just another of the monks who had disappeared years ago.

"Brother Thomas has gone missing," the abbot announced.

"I'm pleased to hear it, abbot, I still ache badly in that shoulder."

"What are your plans? I guess you've had enough here?"

"No, I'll stay around to see what more I can find out; things have happened here that I must resolve."

*　　*　　*

Later, the abbot summons Brother Thomas from his hideaway room to his office.

"*Why did you fail?*" His face reddened with anger.

"He was too quick for me, but he *was* wounded," he explained.

"We must stop him from destroying our mission," the abbot said after a long silence, as Brother Thomas furrowed his brow, straining his already tortured mind to try and come up with a plan of action. "I will poison the professor with the essence of Vril."

"But how will you find any?" questioned the contorting monk.

"Oh, that will be taken care of, don't you worry."

The abbot went up to the abbey roof and waited. Soon, he was spotted by the three ravens who settled in a flurry beside him. They understood his intentions as he quietly spoke to them of his plan and scolded them for their failure to dissect the professor on the mountain slope.

That evening, he and Brother Thomas, armed with powerful torches, went down to the Black Stone Chamber behind the abbey crypt wall after moving the heavy stone slab blocking the entrance way. Once inside, the abbot opened up a large, ornate, oak chest and pulled out an enormous ancient hessian bag. A raw cold draught blew into the chamber from the river opening as the three raven brothers and their crow sister flew in and settled noisily on the chamber floor, freely defaecating with excitement.

Abbot Gregory carefully opened the huge bag and the birds watched him lay out the gigantic black feathered mass upon the polished black granite altar amidst much clicking, cawing and other ungodly utterances. As the mass was unfolded, Brother Thomas helped the abbot swing it over his shoulder and pass his arms through the loop webbing and his head into the hideous black-beaked mask of a monster raven. He stood resplendent before the corvid siblings as he uttered demonic incantations, making swooping movements with his outstretched arms to emulate the raven deity he represented.

The ancient ritual produced expectant deep rumbling vibrations from beneath the altar floor as vapour began to rise up through the central orifice of the altar itself and into the satanic stone-carved chamber. The minutes passed as the grey vapour took on the more substantial form of a humanoid figure that began rising above them, condensing the thick vapour to a liquid essence falling to the floor from the demon's quivering outstretched finger-tips. Strange other-worldly dancing shadows mixed with refractive caustic patterns around the chamber, generated from Brother Thomas' torch beam as it partly passed through the semi-translucent figure.

The abbot produced a small glass vial to collect the precious fluid, being careful not to allow the drops to fall upon his bare hands. The toxic evil miasma was at last at the disposal of the abbot to carry out his plan to use it against the professor. Once corked he held the vial high above him to the cackling applause of the evil black birds who then departed from the chamber and back into the river tunnel from whence they came, as the miasmic demon shrunk back into the black-rimmed annulus back to Hell.

The grotesque raven outfit was ritualistically refolded and returned to its chest and the two men then shifted the stone slab back to its closed position behind them, sealing the evil stone room once again.

Professor Benson spent the next day, again exploring the huge abbey's surroundings, being on his guard for any sign of Brother Thomas. He guessed the monk had gone the way of the others and was never to be seen again.

The little village of Grimsfell was laid out below him like toys on a map, with the cliff line giving way to the seascape beyond without any hint of the raging waters breaking onto the rocky shore below. He wondered how many monks and children may have perished there, and exactly *where* the river flowed out deep beneath the cliff's waterline.

It was a fine day for a welcome meal at The Witch's Brew and the landlord greeted him like a long-lost friend. The professor decided to reveal his ordeal and meeting with Duncan in the hope that it may jog George's memory.

"I often spoke with Duncan about the odd goings-on around here after he'd said he felt unwell; I'm so glad he's alive and well. Are you making headway unravelling the mystery?" asked George.

"I think so, as long as I don't run into Brother Thomas again."

After a long chat about the village history once more, the landlord excused himself to get on with his neglected chores. The professor returned to the abbey the long way by the cliffs, deep in thought about the possible outcome of the planned October corvid assassination attempt with Duncan.

The Halloween Chamber

Back inside he found the abbot in the hallway examining the horrific paintings.

"Those are a bit grim don't you think?" commented the professor.

"They are indeed. A lot of evil things went on in the old days. I often wonder how accurate these depictions are and who decided to display them here, and why."

"Well, I'm absolutely determined to solve our mystery here over the coming weeks, that is if you still require my services?"

"Of course, of course," the abbot repeated without looking up. "I'm under pressure to ensure the turmoil ends; that is why I hired you. Would you join me for a private meal in my study this evening? I'm very interested in your experience in psychiatry and would like to learn a bit about the subject – that is if you don't mind talking shop as it were."

"No, I'll be happy to come along. Would about seven suit you?"

"Seven it is then."

CHAPTER SEVEN

The Poisoning

The professor paused at the paintings as if convinced their detail may hold a clue, or perhaps it was just wishful thinking. He knocked on the abbot's study door, remembering the state he was in the morning after he arrived.

"Come in professor," called the abbot from within.

The small dining table had a centre-piece of chicken surrounded by a few side dishes of vegetables and two bottles of white wine on a floral lace-edged tablecloth.

"The evening staff did a good job don't you think, professor?"

"They certainly did - it looks delicious."

"Well I hope you're hungry after your long walk."

"I will *definitely* enjoy this."

"Pull up a chair and tell me how you got into the psychiatry business."

"Well, my father was a brilliant botanist, but as a child I noticed he wasn't entirely happy and often shut himself away from the rest of the family. Of course, as a child, I thought he was avoiding me for some unknown reason, but as I got older and became interested in botany myself, we became very much closer, and it was then I began to realise he was deeply troubled by something.

"One day I found him in his study with his head in his hands gently sobbing to himself. I immediately rushed over to ask what was the matter - I must have been about fourteen. It was then he confided in me that he felt his work wasn't good enough, not as perfect as he felt it should've been.

"He worked a lot at home on research projects for an agricultural company keen to produce hybridised plants which would be disease resistant and higher yielding, and he was good at it, producing a number of significant scientific papers on the subject based on field trials. However, he always felt they could have been better and dwelt on this worry."

"Were you able to help him realise that his work was worthwhile?"

"I tried, but it was then that I needed to know more about his condition, his state of mind, and started to read up on psychiatry. It became an all-consuming obsession for me to try and help my father out of his unnecessary misery. It was far more important for me to understand his mind, to perhaps enable me to find a way to see him happy and content - more important than the botany."

"That was very admirable of you; did you succeed?"

"Unfortunately not. I just saw him deteriorate whilst understanding why in psychiatric terms; it was frustrating and heartbreaking. He could never accept that his work was excellent – he was always striving to be better, despite the adverse effect it was having on him and his family. We just watched him change for the worse and eventually become bedridden; so it was then I decided I would stick with psychiatry in the hope I may be able to help others out of their misery."

"That is *such* a sad story – I'm so sorry."

To the professor, the abbot was clearly moved, but he had other things on his mind. He opened a bottle and poured out two glasses of wine and then proceeded to wrench off the two greasy chicken legs with unusual vigour, offering one to the professor.

"Please excuse fingers! Help yourself to the vegetables."

The professor was starving by now and tucked into the generous meal he had before him.

The abbot continued: "What happened to your father, did he have to give up his prestigious career?"

"He died . . . and I've never got over it, abbot."

"Tragic. It must have proved to be a very worthy career for you. Were you able to help others as you'd hoped?"

"I did - many people - people who could easily have become like my father, but new medication became available which was a great help, just as long as they didn't have too much of it. Will you excuse me for a minute? I must go to the bathroom."

"Through the door by my trusty old lectern," he pointed.

Professor Benson keeled over and fell headlong into a kaleidoscopic maelstrom of disturbing images, his senses overwhelmed by the onslaught of a deafening cacophony generated by the miasmic essence injected into his chicken leg. His poison-induced terrifying vivid dreams and noisy nightmares now became his reality as he mentally fought to deal with them.

Cascading images slid insidiously into his unconsciousness and manifested themselves as if all his memories of a lifetime's nightmares and real-life terror experiences were available to him, awaiting their turn, uninvited, to re-enact their twisted visions. The powerful essence of Vril heightened this mental experience to a level far greater than that of true reality - a supercharged surreality. Remembered anxiety states overwhelmed his inner senses and applied themselves in a myriad of permutations to torment his raw, naked susceptible mind, denying him control as the evil abbot stood watching him from the doorway.

CHAPTER EIGHT

The Ordeal

Dreams are not always a happy place to be. The professor was dreaming about his father being unhappy – he felt unhappy too. He wasn't comfortable – not physically or mentally – in fact his mind was unable to settle on any aspect of his tangled memory for very long before it history-hopped from one time and place to another.

Waves of electric adrenalised fear pulsed through his body as he reacted to remembered ordeals he had endured in the past. Landscapes, buildings, rooms and faces, distorted in his tortured mind, creating a hideous manifestation of uncertainty.

He cried uncontrollably as he relived the moment he found out his father had died. Perhaps he was only dreaming that he had died and would soon remember the times after his father recovered when they set about botanical research together, enthusiastically writing papers on successfully created hybrids which would help reduce starvation in the poor parts of the world.

He was cold - very cold - and started to shiver on the heat absorbing black granite altar top where he had been incarcerated deep in the bowels of the abbey. He screamed for no particular reason, just because he could or should. A song persisted in his mind – the one his mother used to play on the family piano, a magnificent instrument passed down through the generations of the Benson family. He smiled, remembering how his little brother danced around the piano when his mother changed the tune to 'Here We Go Round the Mulberry Bush' or 'Hey Diddle Diddle'.

He hears his mother calling him in from the garden at tea-time: "Charlie", she *never* called him Charles, but his father *always* did. Each time he hoped it would be crumpets and butter or strawberries and cream after the cucumber and salad cream sandwiches; he didn't like the fish paste sandwiches much at all!

The professor became aware of a rushing sound and a bleak, cold draught as he gradually opened his eyes after briefly regaining consciousness. There was nothing to see. Was he blind or perhaps still in the depths of the garden long after tea-time, playing in the dark old shed pretending to be scared of monsters?

His hands felt around the cold hard stone as he tried to make sense of his situation. Did he dream he had dinner with the abbot? Had he fallen asleep somewhere in the study with a very full stomach? Panic tried to overwhelm him as he resisted and called upon his scientific reasoning and pragmatic constitution. It was then he was aware of a faint flickering light and he sat bolt upright in anticipation. Slowly he made out the shape of a figure emerging from an illuminated arched stone opening a few yards in front of him, holding a torch.

"Professor! Professor! Are you there?"

He recognised the familiar voice of Brother Dawson and

immediately called back with dazed surprise and gratitude.

"I *knew* you would be here," said the brother. "I suspected the abbot was up to no good and listened at his study door last night. Long after you had gone to the bathroom I heard the abbot on the phone asking for assistance. I quickly hid and then followed them carrying you down to the crypt and on through to here."

"Thank goodness you did, brother."

"Much later, I couldn't move the stone to get in here, so I got into the river tunnel by the old Witch's Cave in the middle of the night."

"How on earth did you know where it led and how far?"

"I've been here before, professor," revealed Brother Dawson. "I was afraid the torch would give up on me, but I knew I could feel my way along the tunnel and had paced out how far it would be on the land above. I had to help you, not just as a friend, but as the only person who can put an end to all this evil."

"You're a friend of Duncan who lives in the mountain. He told me you would be my contact over the months before the raid on The Halloween Chamber we've planned for next October."

Despite still reeling from his ordeal, the professor briefly explained the plan Duncan and he had concocted in the mountain retreat and asked Brother Dawson if he would help them.

"Of course I will come along with you both to eradicate the evil Bennetts. When they next assume their vulnerable human form they can die!"

"Well, how the hell are we going to get out of here? I don't feel able to cope with that wet rocky tunnel."

"If you're up to it, we should both be able to move the stone sealing this place off from the crypt, but we must hide you somewhere. The abbot will think you've perished in the cold because you couldn't have moved the stone slab by yourself even if you could've seen it, and your escape by the tunnel was unlikely. I wonder why they hadn't made sure you were dead?"

"Perhaps they wanted it to be the work of the Devil and not be to blame themselves. I guess the abbot must have slipped me a Mickey Finn."

"I first became suspicious of the new abbot about a year after he arrived here. The previous abbot left under odd circumstances which were never entirely explained. Abbot Nicholas was a good man who went on a planned trip to visit his old monastery and never returned. It was said he was taken ill with appendicitis and died during the operation to remove it – but I don't believe it, professor."

"We must get on out of here before your torch gives out. Can you give me a hand off of this bloody cold stone box. I bet the damn thing's hollow with something dreadful inside."

"Best not to ask, professor – best not."

The light from the dimly lit crypt was a welcome sight as they heaved the stone slab open to make their escape. After replacing it, they exited the crypt and the professor followed Brother Dawson up into the vast attic rooms under the abbey roof.

"Is this going to be my hiding place?"

"I'm afraid it's not ideal, but I'm sure you'll be safe up here, that is, as long as you're not scared of bats and spiders!" he chuckled.

It was the first time the professor had witnessed any humour from the little monk who had saved his life.

"Up here was where the monks of old slept; it's now used

for storage. You see those old dusty trunks and racks of robes?"

"They must date back centuries," remarked the professor.

"They do, it's a sort of museum up here now. All sorts of stuff. I brought some clean bedding up here earlier and a jug of water, a bowl and this old bottle to pee in."

"That's very thoughtful of you."

"We can't have you wandering about looking for a lavatory – you might be seen, which could get back to Gregory."

"You've dropped the 'abbot' prefix."

"Damn right! I'm off to bed now myself, I'm very weary. I'll come up to see you sometime tomorrow – although it's already tomorrow. We'll decide then what we'll do with you and I'll contact Duncan for ideas. I guess it may be your best bet to stay in the mountain with him again until the raid on Halloween.

"I'm hoping Gregory doesn't go back to check your body, but he'll just assume you tried to escape by the river tunnel and perished, to be swept out to sea like those devilish monks of old I imagine."

"That's a charming thought, Brother Dawson! Goodnight and thanks."

"Good night, professor."

CHAPTER NINE

The Bone Chamber

Brother Dawson waited until mid-morning before returning to the attic room to find the professor asleep, but decided to awaken him with a gentle tug on the shoulder.

"Oh! My goodness!" the professor exclaimed. "What a terrible bad dream I've just had - I dreamt I was still in that bloody stone room."

"I need to tell you what I discovered yesterday in the Witch's Cave on my way to get you."

"Not a witch I hope!?"

"Bones."

"What type of bones, brother?"

"Human bones - children's bones."

"How did you find them? I thought that cave had been searched long ago."

"It was, several times, but not where I went. I was going down from the main cave to the river through the tunnels when I found myself in a smaller cave - not the river as I'd expected. Although quite a bit smaller, it was still a good-sized cave, and as I shone my torch around the floor I saw the bones, except I thought they were rocks at first."

The Halloween Chamber

"An awful discovery, but at least we know some of the children's remains exist and weren't swept out to sea and lost. Were there any adult bones?"

"None," replied the brother. "But the children's bones weren't in a pile or scattered about - they were arranged in patterns – pentagrams. Those evil hags had laid out the femurs as pentagrams and five skulls were put between their points."

"That's grotesque! Have you told anyone else?"

"No, I wanted your opinion as to what we should do next."

"Well, I would like to see them for myself. Would you take me there?"

"I will, but it's a grim sight I didn't really want to lay eyes on again."

"I do understand, but I want to take photographs of them."

"Are you recovered enough from your ordeal for us to go there this afternoon?"

"I think so – I'm keen to keep up the momentum and get this thing properly investigated. If I ever get away from this place I will write it all up as a paper or even a book – but no-one will ever believe it."

After lunch Brother Dawson sneaked some food back to the professor and they went down to his room to collect his camera, then out through a side door unnoticed, down to the sea cliffs below.

"Watch your step when we get to the rocks," warned the brother. I turned over my ankle yesterday, but luckily didn't strain anything, otherwise you may still be in that godless chamber."

"Perish the thought," shuddered the professor.

The Halloween Chamber

It was yet another dull, grey, windy day as they headed for Lovers' Crag where the Witch's Cave lay beneath. The cave entrance was well hidden, only visible once inside a deep fissure on the cliff face, perilously close to a near-vertical drop to the rocks below. Lovers throughout history met on the large ledge twenty feet or so above, unaware they were within the power of the witches who craved the power of the young girls' lustful passion to insidiously sap from them to turn them into crones and witches to make up their numbers. Brother Dawson led the way.

"That's some drop to the sea, brother. How did you manage to get here in the dark just by torchlight?"

"He must nedys go that the deuell dryues."

"What was that?"

"Needs must when the devil drives. I had no choice; I had to save you."

"And I'm very grateful you did too, Brother Dawson."

"If we get through here it opens out inside," he instructed the professor. "It then gets easier for a while."

Sure enough the Witch's Cave revealed itself in the same manner as Duncan's cave. A vast limestone cave filled with artifacts from long ago: old chairs and rough beds; dilapidated cupboards and piles of battered pots and pans beside a long redundant blackened hearth hewn into the rock floor and wall.

"Do you know how long a coven existed here?"

"For well over a thousand years they reckon. Alice Bennett was just one in a long line of crones who took to the dark side in response to persecution, just because they were clever at cures and so-called spells. They were considered in league with the Devil because of their apparent supernatural powers, but they were just intelligent women who didn't wish to mix with ordinary folk and lived their lives in a group of like-minded women. Persecution creates revenge, so they took to using their powers to lure young girls into their coven and to kidnapping the children of those families who had sought to decimate them."

"How did you learn all these things?"

"From the Grimsfell elders who passed on the stories over the centuries. George Morgan at the pub has collected the stories, but who knows if they're true or not? Stories can become changed completely after many tellings with false embellishments added along the way."

"That's also my thinking, otherwise it all seems just too fantastic to be true; but he found old papers buried in the wall which supports the stories. Your discovery of the pentagram bones are surely highly significant then, unless someone is raiding old graves to perpetrate a hoax! Where are the bones then?"

"On the way down to the river – I'll show you when I catch my breath."

At the far end of the Witch's Cave, a narrow, low tunnel continued for many yards until it sloped steeply downwards. Brother Dawson shone his light down whilst the professor used his to look back at where they had come, to reassure himself they could get back if anything untoward happened. They became aware of a cold draught and a distant roaring the further they descended – a sure sign the river was near.

"Somewhere near the bottom of this shaft I took a turning away from the river tunnel without realising it. That's when I discovered the Bone Chamber, as I call it," explained the brother with a tone of anticipation colouring his voice. "Have you got your film wound on and your flash bulbs ready?"

"Yes. All set and ready to capture this vital piece of evidence," said the eager professor fiddling with his flash gun.

"I'm sure it's somewhere near here. Ah Ha! . . ."

Following the brother through yet another tight gap, the torchlight lit up the scene: laid out before them in the centre of the chamber were the pentagrams, exactly as he had described them. Each arrangement had five skulls neatly placed between the vertices formed by the fifteen femurs with a central pentagon making up the inverted pentagrams. The professor took out his camera and screwed in the first flash bulb, then adjusted the focus and exposure settings on the lens turret according to his light meter, using the limited light from both their steadied torches.

"I hope the flash works."

"It should, with the new Ever Readys fitted."

With bated breath he pressed down the shutter lever which resulted in a blinding, but satisfying flash, much to their relief. The completed twelve exposures committed the many bone pentagrams to film and were then safely wound on to the uptake spool.

"We're not going back to the abbey along the river," said the professor. He meant it as a statement rather than a question.

"No, I don't fancy repeating that just now either."

It took a good hour to exhaustively climb back up the way they had come and on out of the Witch's Cave back on to the cliff face path to the top. They walked a little further along the cliff to the little path which ran down to Lovers' Crag and sat down for a well-earned rest before attempting the rising landscape up to the abbey when a shot rang out, echoing around the crags.

The Halloween Chamber

"I'm hit!" gasped the professor grasping the brother's arm. "Let's get out of here."

They were on their feet in seconds as two more shots were fired. With quick-thinking reactions the professor held up his camera to face the gunman, who ran off fearing his picture would incriminate him.

"That was a good idea!" said the relieved brother.

"It *was* wasn't it." agreed the professor. "Did you see who it was?"

"Put it like this: Brother Thomas is no longer a missing person."

"I thought that bugger would have another go at me."

CHAPTER TEN

Respite

Dusk was imminent and it was clear neither of them could return to the abbey, so it was decided the best option was to turn up at The Witch's Brew and talk to George. Brother Dawson helped the ailing professor across the difficult hillside as the light faded. In the distance the village lights beckoned and soon the intrepid duo staggered into the pub and sat on the nearest bench.

"Where is everyone?" remarked the professor, scanning the darkened scene for any signs of life.

"It's early yet for the evening crowd."

George had heard the commotion as they bustled through the door and hastened down the stairs.

"Hello? Business starting early tonight?"

"It's Professor Benson and my friend Brother Dawson, George. Can you give us a hand?"

"Well, what've *you two* been up to then?"

"Things are hotting up, George. We've just been shot at by one of the demented brothers. We've been cave hunting under the Witch's Cave and I have photos proving some very nasty goings-on down there that Brother Dawson here discovered yesterday: bones - children's bones - laid out in pentagrams," puffed the professor.

George's face changed from surprised amusement to concerned worry as they helped the professor over to an easy chair in the corner.

"Food? . . . Drink? . . . What can I get you both?"

"A drink of your best brew will be just the thing, George; I'll eat after I've told you what's been happening since I last saw you."

"OK prof - take your time, then I must look at that wound."

"You're not going to believe this, but the bloody abbot's in on this, along with some of his deranged monks. I was drugged by Gregory at a meal he invited me to and ended up on a stone altar in a devilish chamber next to the crypt – Brother Dawson here saved me."

"Nothing surprises me now, prof; it all seems to be coming to a head."

"The latest missing monk and Gregory are out to get me – I know too much, George. We can't go back to the abbey and I'm hoping you might be able to put us up here for a while."

"Well of course, it's the least I can do; there's a good-sized room at the back, if you don't mind sharing."

"Thanks George, that'll be fine. Now I must get some rest."

George discovers the professor got away with only a graze and daubed it with tincture of iodine, all wrapped up in a bandage.

"That's very professional, thanks. Don't 'alf sting though!"

He shows the professor to the room and Brother Dawson stays at the bar to speak with the landlord on his return.

"I *must* contact Duncan, George, to tell him all that's happened and start making definite plans for Halloween; I just wish there were more of us involved."

"I may be able to help you there, brother," encouraged George. "When the prof first came to the pub he bought an old man a drink, and that man is Gabriel Fleming, the grandfather of Florence, the latest child to go missing from the village. He is too frail to help, but his daughter, Florence's mother, has spoken of her desire to be a part of anything which will throw light on her daughter's disappearance. Not only her, but also Rose, Rose Bennett, who has become her friend over the years."

"So we could have two women along with us who have a vested interest in the destruction of the Bennett siblings." The brother spoke his thoughts out loud: "It looks like the force of good is building against the force of evil."

"Very philosophical," commented George.

"Do Rose and this man's daughter come in here often?"

"Very rarely, because of the pub's name. It's not a place they want to be associated with, along with its witchy themes, although Gabriel isn't bothered. Florence's mother is Abigail Fleming, she never married and calls herself Gail."

"I'll speak with the prof tomorrow, it seems our little death squad is growing in numbers."

Brother Dawson thanks George and retires to bed.

In the early hours, all the pub's occupants are awakened by strong gusts of wind and crashing sounds outside. At the window Brother Dawson could make out various objects taking flight, lifted by the wind.

"Sounds bad out there, brother," said the prof, half asleep.

He didn't reply, but stood by the window lost deep in thought. It was as though dark forces were gathering to deny the intentions they harboured against them.

In the morning, a knock at their door revealed George holding a tray of steaming hot tea and toast for them - a welcome sight. After a while the brother told the prof about Rose and Gail.

"It's far too dangerous for women; I can't allow it!" he blurted.

"I think you'll have a big fight on your hands if you don't, prof."

"Maybe so, but I'm responsible for everyone's safety," insisted the professor.

"I'm not so sure about that! Rose and Gail have reasons of their own to come along – more reason in fact than either of us."

"We must meet with them as soon as we can to explain just exactly what our dangerous mission involves. They'll change their minds *then*."

When George arrived back with his daily provisions he found the two of them seated at the big table by the bar, poring over sheets of paper.

"Plans, gentlemen?" he asked.

"Yep! We've got to get things organised before we meet up with the ladies. Should we call at one of their houses?" the professor enquires.

"No. I have to go out again soon. You can't afford to be seen outside or you'll get the dangerous duo on your trail again."

"OK, thanks George, you're right."

Late afternoon after dark, George arrives with Rose and Gail. The professor stood up. "Rose, we meet again, and Gail."

"I heard about your ordeal from George; we will put a stop to this and follow your plans," Rose said glancing to Gail, "and we'll both be there with you to see it's done, professor."

The Halloween Chamber

"Ladies, I do hope you both fully realise just how dangerous this task will be and that your lives will be at risk," warned the professor.

"But that fact will not stop us both from taking part."

"You seem very determined."

"You bet! Gail must know what happened to Florence and stop it happening again to another child. My wicked ancestors, Alice and her brothers, will die once and for all; I will personally see to it if needs be – it's now my duty."

"We plan to use fire as the only certain means to kill them, Rose – flame-throwers no less."

"Sounds good to me. I'll use one if I have to."

All the team were gathered at the big table passing sheets of notes between them and adding ideas, all that is, except the absent Duncan. Just before midnight they all stood and held hands in a circle of determined intention to successfully fulfill their task ahead. George suddenly pushed in to link hands with the circle, announcing that he too would join them.

The Halloween Chamber

CHAPTER ELEVEN

Abduction

Christmas passed, thankfully without the loss of another child, as the team celebrated the New Year in the privacy of George's living room, again reaffirming their dedication. This time Duncan was there with them to complete the team of six.

February was unusually cold and bleak at Grimsfell with the ominous distant lights from the abbey a constant reminder of the task ahead. The professor and Brother Dawson passed the days discussing psychiatry, and this time the professor's words were received with genuine interest, not as before as abbot Gregory's lure.

Amidst one of their many late night chess games, the wind arose with the crashing they had heard last time. Determined not to let it spoil their game, the two each intensified their determination to win. The professor had a check-mate lined up and was ready to pounce with his knight.

The door burst open with an enormous crash causing the professor's knee-jerk reaction to explosively scatter the pieces from the chess board, as in rushed two hooded figures wielding knives. Before they could begin defending themselves, the two were overpowered by the dark assailants and pulled to the floor amongst the remains of their game. The last they knew was sweet chloroform filling their lungs.

George was away overnight at his brother's house in a nearby village, a fact which must have prompted the attack. Brother Dawson awoke first to the intense cold and nearby roar of water in the Halloween Chamber – the focus of all their plans. The unconscious professor yet to realise their perilous situation.

"We have you at last, Benson." The unmistakable voice of abbot Gregory, but infused with condescending overtones which drew the professor out of his chemically induced slumber.

"You evil bastard!" exploded the professor. "Where's Brother Dawson?"

"Here with you – also trapped and defeated, professor," quipped the smug Gregory. "Now you'll pay the price for meddling in our business."

"But you *asked* me to come here and do just that."

"I had to keep up respectable appearances and be seen by my monks that I cared and was concerned for them, and that I was actively seeking professional help. It's all become clear at last now, hasn't it professor?" he said sarcastically.

"Very clear Gregory. Go back to Hell!"

"All in good time professor. First we have work to do making you and Dawson here suffer for your deeds before we dispose of you for good."

"Bad choice of words, Gregory, not for *good*, but for *evil*."

"Very amusing, but I must admit you are right."

The cold was becoming unbearable as the professor and

The Halloween Chamber

Brother Dawson took in their surroundings in that evil stone chamber. They were each secured and propped-up against the sloping walls of adjacent alcoves, the chamber by now dimly lit by daylight from the central aperture, part of the old well shaft above them.

Gregory and Thomas had positioned themselves in the remaining alcoves opposite and focussed their attention on the vent in the centre of the floor which they all partly encircled. Gregory took out his little bottle of miasmic Vril which had previously been used to drug the professor and leant forwards to allow a few drops to descend into the annulus, smiling at Thomas as he resumed his reclining position. They both began chanting and gesticulating as the minutes passed. Then, accompanied by a hideous deep rumbling, just a faint whisp at first developed at an alarming rate into a vertical, shimmering cloud as a demon materialised before them, forced from its slumbers in Hell through the membrane dividing the two worlds: the world above and the dark evil world beneath – an early, angry awakening requiring tremendous effort to rip the membrane so easily ruptured on All Hallows' Eve.

A sense of achievement was evident on the faces of those who summoned and frozen horror on the others who witnessed it.

"*Now* is the time," uttered Gregory through clenched teeth, emulated by Thomas' maniacal grin of anticipation.

The demon evolved into a more substantial form and then fragmented into miasmids accompanied by deep bass tones and vibration from the ground beneath their feet. Coloured miasmids swirled ever outwards towards all those assembled in the chamber, like a galaxy in torment.

With eyes closed in intense expectation, all four were not

sure what was to happen next, but what *did* happen was entirely unexpected: Duncan appeared in the opening to the river tunnel.

Events transformed from swirling, energy-draining terror to a calm peace as the demon quickly descended back into the vent from whence it came, like a frightened rabbit scurrying back into its burrow. It was clear Duncan had a power greater than the emanations from Hell!

Duncan stood to one side as Gregory and Thomas made their hurried escape into the river tunnel.

"Don't let them go, Duncan!" called out the frantic professor.

"They're harmless now their power's been taken from them; now let's untie you and get you out of here. I'll explain later."

The two bewildered men followed Duncan back up the tunnel to the mountain cave and the relative comfort and safety of Duncan's improvised living room where he revealed his story of how he acquired his awesome power.

"I am visited by ghosts, gentlemen. At first I thought I must be dreaming, but gradually I had to accept the truth. The souls of tormented monks, young girls who died as witches and the Christmas Children of Grimsfell, all visit me through the river tunnel. It acts as a dimension portal from the 'good dead' to the 'good living'.

"They have a remarkable energy drawn from the power of good. It overwhelms evil, and I have some of their power bestowed to me - stored within me for when I may need it – it's their gift to me; I used it at the Chamber."

"It's difficult to believe, but I've seen it with my own eyes with Brother Dawson as a witness," admitted the astonished professor. "This, then, is our weapon, Duncan."

"Not on its own against the corvids."

"Why not?"

"Because they're immune through their immortality of reincarnation. They gave up human form for their continued eternal existence as corvids to escape death by flight, and in doing so are protected from any powers which would otherwise threaten them, except, that is, when they give way to temptation on Halloween and relish their brief return to mortal human form.

"For this privilege they are compelled to conjure the Demon of Revenge to replenish the miasma which influences susceptible good monks in the abbey to become evil recruits in their cause. You're right that fire is the only means to their permanent destruction during the brief time when they're human again, but, the presence of my power *will* act as a catalyst for the power of good to succeed - like throwing petrol on the fire so to speak. I will be there for you on that day to ensure the destruction of the evil, and to put the souls who visit me at peace."

Grateful to Duncan for saving their lives, they settled down to an uneasy sleep in makeshift beds with crowded minds on the verge of nightmares.

The Halloween Chamber

CHAPTER TWELVE

Plans

His fitful sleep was a strange affair for the professor, mumbling and shouting throughout as he relived the recent events that tormented him. Many times Brother Dawson was at his side with his hand on his shoulder to gently comfort him and to tell him it was over and that they were all safe; in a way, he was relieved that he *didn't* sleep.

Duncan slept with a knowing confidence that all this madness could soon be over, just as long as he was there as insurance. Later the next day he was up before the others organising more comfortable living conditions until they could return to The Witch's Brew.

"Duncan! Did I dream your story about the power of souls within you?"

"Professor! Did you finally get some rest?" replied Duncan, surprised at the sudden voice.

"I don't really know. Everything's like a living nightmare at the moment; I fear I'm going mad, Duncan."

"You'll be fine once you're back at George's place."

During their return to comparative normality, the professor and Brother Dawson made sure they were never at the pub alone, and if George had to be away then they would accompany him, stealthily.

* * *

Spring was soon in the air, leaving the depressing dark winter months behind, just as the morning light dispels bad dreams. Rose and Gail made a point of regularly visiting Brother Dawson and the professor at The Witch's Brew to keep all their spirits up. Rose was growing increasingly fond of the professor but kept it to herself.

Questions were put to the village abbey workers for clues as to what was going on, but to no avail. Everyone watched out for wandering monks, but none were seen. Once the locals had learned of George's lodgers, business at The Witch's Brew improved dramatically with the professor gaining mild celebrity status. Rose and Gail kept to themselves with increasing anxiety about the success of the October plan always on their minds. Duncan called every few weeks to spend the night at the pub to discuss developments.

After the discovery of the children's Pentagram Bones, as they came to be known, the police and archaeologists removed the bones from below the Witch's Cave to be buried in the village cemetery amidst great ceremony and grieving. Centuries before, the village dead were interred at the abbey cemetery, but as the village grew larger an area of land between the village and the sea cliffs was consecrated and used as a cemetery instead. The femurs and skulls were placed in a purpose-built vault named *The Vault of the Christmas Children*. Their lost bones remained to be discovered.

The Halloween Chamber

As the bone cave was so close to the underground river's submarine exit, demands from villagers resulted in a search for more remains at the site, it being organised with divers in the region contacted for their help. It was decided that the search would start on May Day, in more clement weather, because the coastal currents and rocks were treacherous at the best of times.

Attempts were first made to reach the tunnel's end from below the Witch's Cave rather than from the sea, but the tunnel terminated abruptly in a seawater-filled hole open to the sea above. A geologist knowledgeable in limestone petrology was consulted, and it became clear the tunnel had been truncated by an ancient, now submerged sink-hole. The tunnel evidently extended much further out under the sea-bed and at some time in the distant past its eroded roof had collapsed at that point into the tunnel and was now open to the sea. Further investigation of the rocks, silt and debris at the bottom of this hole which now blocked the further reaches of the tunnel, revealed hundreds of human bones of all ages: men, women and children – the children's lost bones.

News of this gruesome discovery was met with a mixture of horror and relief by the villagers, but the relatives of the men – the lost monks - had yet to learn of their discovery. Discussion was under-way at the village hall, led by Rose and Gail, as to whether the villagers' remains should stay where they were or be retrieved and buried in the village cemetery, with the children's remains placed alongside the Pentagram Bones of the Christmas Children.

Rose Bennett's house was situated at the most ancient end of Grimsfell, near to where the path diverged up to the abbey by the seven trees to the left and down to the sea cliffs to the right. During the early summer months Rose was often seen pottering around in her garden; she seemed much happier with the professor on her mind. Some folks said hello, others didn't - because of her surname. The days of witches was long gone, but it seemed impossible for the relatives of lost daughters and children not to feel Rose had evil in her blood. It seemed certain the demonic monks were guilty of recent child abductions, but the evil link was always there in the minds of many and she continued to be eyed with doubt and suspicion.

*   *   *

One bright June morning Rose was tending to her vegetable garden when something prompted her to look up – she froze to the spot as a large crow perched on the garden fence staring intensely at her. Of course Rose knew the story of her ancestor Alice's reincarnation as a crow - was she now in her presence? Instinctively, Rose spoke:

"Hello Alice, your days are numbered," she said half in nervous humour, trying to get the supernatural thoughts out of her head.

The huge black bird left its perch and rattled the fence as it did so, to circle overhead and then dive towards Rose. She screamed and covered her head with her hands, but the crow's sturdy beak punched into Rose's head. Before the bird flew off, two more swooping attacks left her unconscious and bleeding, to be seen by the many folk who passed by on that busy sunny morning; they had heard her screams and witnessed the continuing attack. Taken into her house, Gail was called.

"Rose! . . . Rose! . . . Wake up!" she pleaded to her friend as she gently wiped her head wounds. Rose slowly regained consciousness and began to stare around the room and then up at Gail.

"She's out to get me, Gail . . . She knows my intentions."

"*Who's* out to get you, Rose?"

"Alice . . . It was bloody Alice . . . the witch!"

"You believe the stories then, Rose?"

"I do now. It's too much of a coincidence, don't you think?"

"I really don't know, but so many strange things happen around here . . . it seems to make sense in that context," conceded Gail. "I have to call the doctor to look at these wounds."

News of the bizarre attack spread quickly around the village, and soon after the doctor left, Professor Benson was at her bedside.

"Are you certain you still want to take part, Rose?"

"Even more so, professor."

"How did I guess you'd say that, Rose?"

"Because you know me well enough by now."

"I guess so."

George arrived with Brother Dawson laden with assorted fruit and stared down at Rose's wounds; he couldn't bring himself to utter a word – his reaction was mirrored in his face.

"The doctor's sure Rose's skull isn't fractured. Crows are powerful birds, but ravens are bigger and meaner," the professor added with authority born of experience. "We have just over three months to plan this correctly, to ensure we end this perpetual revenge quest. These evil immortals will prove to be very mortal if we get this right and strike in their window of susceptibility."

"Duncan has seen the ritual twice and knows pretty much how long we'll have to fry them," Brother Dawson said reassuringly.

The Halloween Chamber

Grim's Fell 'neath Oros, to give the ancient little village its original name, looked idyllic in the June sunshine. The dominant mountain backdrop and the eerie abbey above the village were much less foreboding and threatening at this time of year, unlike late October with its menacing overtones as darker evenings heralded winter gloom.

A particularly warm and busy lunchtime saw The Witch's Brew buzzing with lively activity. Duncan was visiting and all the team were enjoying the fresh summer air over jugs of George's Special Brew, which, legend has it, George concocts in the depths of his ancient cellar in a huge black cauldron with ear of bat, leg of frog and wart of toad. Disturbingly, he never denied it!

Rose was healing well, with only a few missing tufts of her jet-black hair missing as evidence of the attack. She felt particularly cheerful sitting next to the professor, sharing his jokes and comparing wounds. Occasionally, he would sense Rose's attention on *him* rather than the other local men. It was as if she trusted him implicitly to end the horrors in the village and abbey and to lift the Bennett curse she felt was upon her and which isolated her in many respects. All her relatives had left the village long ago fearing for their safety, to find alternative anonymous residence far away from Grimsfell.

At first, no-one spotted the three ravens circling above, but when someone did, the happy atmosphere instantly descended into fearful silence as all eyes turned skyward.

"They're keeping an eye on us," the professor said, breaking the silence and inducing nervous chuckles from the gathering.

"Well, they'd better keep their distance while I get my

shotgun," said John the gardener, provoking a sudden rush of men to leap to their feet to do likewise.

"You *can't* kill them!" exclaimed a voice from the back.

"We'll see about that," said another, turning from his dash to his house.

Then, with all eyes upon them, the three ravens simply vanished from the clear blue summer sky in full view of everyone present.

"That's proof they're supernatural and really *are* the three Bennett brothers for sure," decided an emphatic Brother Dawson.

As the late evening drew to a close and the pub gradually emptied, dusk fell uneasily on the good folk of Grimsfell. Although a warm night, many closed their shutters and locked their doors, uncertain what this particular night may bring. Loaded shotguns were propped up by back doors and windows by those who hoped they could bag a raven or two – or three.

The abbey bell seemed eternal as it chimed away the day's twelve hours, as if signalling to the village that the next few hours of darkness would be perilous. Few slept that night.

Abbot Gregory had again donned his raven outfit, flapping and swooping majestically upon the abbey roof with Brother Thomas looking on admiringly. The minutes passed, until, one by one, the immortal raven brothers alighted before him. Then Alice arrived to complete the evil band. Gregory spoke:

"We have work to do brothers and sister," he began.

A cacophony of cackles filled the night air as the corvids bobbed up and down in agitated agreement.

The Halloween Chamber

CHAPTER THIRTEEN

Revelation

After an uneventful few days, all was back to normal as the village returned to daily life, albeit with eyes darting skyward at the least opportunity.

The professor was stretched out on a garden recliner digesting his mid-day meal in the pub's back garden as Rose Bennett made her way through the village from her cottage with a determined but worried look on her face.

"Hello Rose," greeted George, who was out the front busy as usual sorting out his baskets of daily provisions. "Are you well?"

"Sort of OK, George, just a lot on my mind. Is the prof about?"

"He's probably asleep out the back - he usually is at this time of day."

"I'll see if he's awake, I need to talk."

"Anything to eat or drink, Rose?"

"No thanks, George."

Rose stood silently thinking at the side of the pub as she gathered up thoughts before she spoke to the professor. Spotting him under the pub's only tree, she called out.

"Hello! . . . Hello! . . . Professor - are you awake?"

On hearing her voice he pushed himself up on his arms to greet her; he'd grown to like her voice as well as her attractive features.

"Rose, how are you my dear? Lovely to see you."

"And you, professor; are you sure I'm not interrupting your after-dinner nap?"

"I'm glad you're here to be honest, Rose. I only keep going over the plans when I'm resting on my own."

"Well, I'm in a similar state at the moment, particularly in view of what I've recently learned from a friend."

"Sounds intriguing, Rose, is it something you wish to share with me?"

"That's why I've come along to see you professor – I need to talk, if that's all right with you?"

"Of course," he replied, jumping to his feet to drag a chair over. "Sit yourself down, I'm a good listener."

"I know you are. There's not many people I can confide in, only Gail. In fact the friend I'm speaking of first approached Gail to say she was ill with guilt and torment about something which happened while she was working at the abbey."

"There's quite a few villagers work up there I gather."

"Yes, mainly women in the laundry and room cleaners with a few men helping the brothers tend the vegetable garden out the back at this time of year. Mary was a room cleaner for some of the monk's sitting rooms and bedrooms at the residential far end of the abbey."

"*Was* a room cleaner you say?"

"Exactly. She's been attacked . . . and there are others."

"Tell me what happened, Rose."

"Our friend, Mary, had cleaned in that area for years and

the monks were always pleasant to her, often asking her about one thing or another. But one November, a couple of years back, one of the monks locked his door and kept the key while they were both in his room and began acting in a very peculiar way, scaring her.

"Mary described how he began chanting in some gibberish and moving his arms around while holding an ornate silvery ring. She was terrified to be stuck in that room with him, professor, and after a few minutes he overpowered her despite her desperate screams and . . . and . . . then he raped her."

Rose broke down in tears with the professor comforting her with his arm around her shoulders, acutely aware of her scent.

"My god, Rose, he became one of the mad monks affected by the Halloween miasma I guess. Then what happened? How did she get away?"

"He threatened her. He said if she told anyone what had happened he would put a curse on her. Now, Mary is quite superstitious, especially in view of what's been happening in the village over the years. She was scared and promised never to reveal what he'd done to her.

"There's more: Mary told Gail that she was ashamed that she'd stolen that ring from the monk in her anger. Earlier, he had been gloating over it during his chanting, pushing and pulling it violently on his fingers. He said he'd stolen it from the abbot, so she thought she would return it to him – but she didn't because she was disturbed by its form and markings. She gave the ring to Gail who gave it to me – I have it here. She just had to confide in someone, and it was Gail. Gail told me yesterday and thought you should know about Mary's experience too."

The Halloween Chamber

"Were there others?"

"Mary is sure there were, because around that time some of her fellow workers were not their usual chatty selves."

"Oh my goodness, Rose, I just hope we can finish all this in a few months time. Can I see the ring?"

"Of course, I brought it for you to see what you made of it."

She unwrapped the silver ring from her handkerchief and gave it to the professor.

"It's disturbing, quite sinister in fact, with its prominent skull and strange symbols around it."

He reached in his pocket for his set of little magnifying glasses, neatly held in a black Bakelite fold-out group of three; he selected the middle one and proceeded to examine the ring. He was silent for a long time, until Rose thought she'd better ask what he thought.

"What do you reckon, professor; do you think it's valuable?"

"Not because it's silver, but because of its origin and what it represents," he said slowly. "Did you see the inscription inside?"

"I noticed some writing, but didn't read it."

"This is a SS Death's Head ring belonging to Hans Kammler and engraved with the signature of Heinrich Himmler in his spiky writing," he explained.

"Well, I've heard of Himmler, but not Kammler. Do you think it's significant that the names are so similar?"

"It so happens that part of my job involved looking into Nazi psychology. In fact it later became the thesis I presented, so I know both names and about the rings being presented to SS officers of distinction by Himmler."

"Who was Hans Kammler then, was he important?"

"He certainly was! He was the officer in charge of building

the extermination camps as well as Hitler's so-called Wunderwaffens – Wonder Weapons."

"How ever did Abbot Gregory get hold of the ring then?"

"Perhaps our Abbot Gregory isn't who we think he is."

He took her hand and suggested a cliff-top walk. Together they slowly walked along the winding path past the cemetery between the village and the sea and on towards the nearby cliffs on this beautiful sunny June afternoon. He occasionally returned his arm around her shoulders and her long black hair as they touched on sensitive areas in their lives:

"Did you ever marry, Rose?" he asked quietly.

"Very nearly, but my fiancé was killed in a motorcycle accident on the road the other side of Oros."

"I'm *so* sorry, Rose."

"I didn't ever really want anyone else after that. What about you professor, have you a wife back home in the city?"

"Once, a while ago now, but like you I lost the love of my life. It leaves an awful empty space I can't fill, even though I try to throw myself into my work it never goes away, especially in the quiet times when I'm on my own. It must be the same for you, Rose?"

They had stopped walking and he had inadvertently moved his hand to hold her head. Rose looked up into his eyes and the moment was right for their kiss. From then on a happiness neither had known for too long overwhelmed them both as they slowly walked back to her cottage arm in arm.

"Rose. I've lost all track of time! I've just remembered I planned to meet up with Duncan at four."

Rose rushed in to check her mantle clock.

"You'll just make it prof. By the way, I don't know your first name?"

The Halloween Chamber

Professor Benson was already hurrying away, but turned and called: "It's Charles . . . or Charlie."

"See you tomorrow, Charlie, at The Witch's Brew."

"Look forward to it, Rose." He blew her a kiss.

CHAPTER FOURTEEN

Intrigue

Duncan was waiting: "Charlie! You mustn't run at your age."

"I'm good for a few more years yet, Duncan. What's been happening?"

"Quite a bit. A woman's been seen in the abbey grounds a brother told me on my way down - and more than once!"

"What did he say?"

"Just gave me his description of her: Youngish and with spectacularly long blonde hair."

"*Really*! That *is* unusual. You're sure he hadn't been drinking!?"

"Don't think so - he didn't smell and wasn't slurring."

"Wishful thinking then?"

"Ha! The thing is, that she appears to be living there, because he said another brother had seen her some months before and they didn't believe *him* either - and there's more."

"More about this woman?"

"Well, not yet, but I'm sure someone'll be hot foot on the trail! I've heard they're still searching that sink hole for bones."

"I thought they'd decided it was best to leave them there."

"No decision on that yet apparently, but they've found a sort of metal wall which was alongside tons of debris they cleared out of the way."

"A *metal* wall!?" exclaimed the professor. "Whatever do they mean by that?"

"The story going round the village is that further investigation will continue soon, weather permitting and if the current allows. I'm surprised you haven't heard all about it."

"I've been out walking this afternoon so I haven't seen many people," explained the professor.

"Most of the search team divers are in the pub now, telling everyone about the mystery."

"It must be a sunken ship if it's metal. Can't think what else it could be, a plane perhaps, but being so close to the village someone would've seen or heard something."

"You'd think so. Come on, I'll buy you a drink."

The Witch's Brew was packed with people, many of which the professor had never seen before. A pile of diving equipment was by the door and the team were trying to explain what they had found in response to the many questions.

"The metal isn't steel," one chap kept repeating. "It's not magnetic and *not* aluminium – we just can't identify it."

"We hope to see more of it in the next few weeks and what it's attached to," added another diver, swigging at his well-earned pint.

"Sounds intriguing," said the professor as he and Duncan tried to get closer to the group.

"A lot of planes went missing off this coast during the war," Duncan enthusiastically informed the group within earshot.

"But I'm sure it's much too shallow for a ship to be hidden there."

"Duncan, I need your help."

"What had you in mind, professor?"

"I want to go back to that creepy mausoleum to check something, but I need a hand."

"To check what?"

"A chest I saw in one of the alcoves; it's often played on my mind as to what may be in it, especially since I've learned some very interesting facts from an item Rose brought me to look at."

The professor recounted his meeting with Rose about the rape and the ring.

"That's very weird stuff; what do you expect to find?"

"I don't know, Duncan, but I have a strong hunch I must respond to. Can you help?"

"Yes, of course; when do you want to do this?"

"After dark – tomorrow OK, Duncan?"

"Fine by me, I'll stay over tonight. How about getting into the old place? Weren't the doors locked up again?"

"Not very securely from what I saw; just new padlocks on a couple of new hasps. There's nothing known of to protect down there as far as anyone is aware, except perhaps that iron-banded chest. I'm intrigued because it looked very sturdy, as if it holds something valuable. I'll see if I can borrow some bolt cutters, George'll know, if he hasn't any himself."

The two met outside the mausoleum just after nightfall the next day, the professor armed with bolt-cutters and two torches.

"Did anyone see you?" asked Duncan.

"Don't think so; I went around the long way and approached from back there." He pointed to where the coastline indented to a little bay.

"Can we get these padlocks off without the torches do you reckon? Don't want to arouse any suspicions," said Duncan, looking back towards the abbey.

"We can feel the lock loops into the cutters; I just hope they're not hardened."

After a few minutes work the locks were off and they pulled open one of the old oak doors, dragging up the grassy soil. With both torches switched on, they moved into the area above the stone steps leading down between the balustrades.

"It's weird in here. Remember where it was?" quipped Duncan.

"Not really, but I think it wasn't up here. Watch out on the way down, there's centuries of bits and pieces on the steps."

Their torchlight revealed the twelve arched alcoves on either side of the lower long room, mirroring the ground floor above, except this level was hewn from the limestone.

"*There* it is, Duncan!" exclaimed the professor. "I'm very glad I hadn't mentioned it to Gregory at the time, but I'm now guessing he knew it was there and had hoped *I* didn't see it."

"Could be."

"Damn! No crowbar," erupted the professor, just as Duncan pulled one out from his rucksack.

"I guessed we'd need it."

The large oak chest was covered with dust and dirt and they wiped away the area around a complicated looking brass lock.

"This *is* interesting – some sort of combination lock by the looks of it, much more recent than the chest itself. We'll try to crack the numbers rather than use the crowbar."

Duncan agreed: "The crowbar won't do much good on *this* box anyhow – it's too heavily armoured with iron."

Cleaning away more dirt with his trusty handkerchief, the professor revealed a large brass base-plate with the letters ABUS engraved upon it, together with three symbols set in an inverted triangle above a six numbered brass rotary combination lock.

"Look at this! Some Greek letters and an *e.*"

"An *e*?" queried Duncan.

"Yep! an *e* . . . and a *pi* . . . and another maths symbol which I'll need to look up."

After several futile attempts to guess the six digits it was decided they would try and lift the chest out and up to Duncan's lair. It took the best part of an hour to get the chest to the top of the steps and out into the night air as they sat on it catching their breath. Being a two-handed job each, they had to hold their torches awkwardly in their mouths to see where they were going.

"I'm not going to get this thing much further," panted the professor.

"No, nor me. I'll go on ahead in a minute and get a rope, but it'll take me around half an hour to get to my cave and I'm out of breath."

"How will the rope help?"

"We can sit the chest on my upturned old dining room table and pull the damned thing along, but I'll have to take the legs off again to get it through the cave entrance."

"How will you get it down here?"

"I'll drag it with the rope."

"OK, if you're happy doing that."

"It's dragging the chest that'll be the hard bit, but we'll do it in stages – we've got all night!"

The Halloween Chamber

Duncan set off with his torch and the professor pulled up his collar against the chilly night air.

His mind wandered to Rose as he reflected on their blossoming relationship and his first kiss in a long time. If he hadn't agreed to this abbey job he would never have met her. His thoughts turned to her insistence she came along on Halloween for the corvid kill, as he greatly feared she may come to harm, the very last thing he wanted. Perhaps he could convince her that it wasn't such a good idea after all nearer the time.

In what seemed a far shorter period of time than he had anticipated, he heard Duncan dragging his table top over the bumpy ground towards him.

"Over here, Duncan."

"Give us a hand prof - have I been gone long?"

"No . . . I don't think so, I was deep in thought."

Soon they had the chest and its unknown contents lashed on to Duncan's upside-down table top with the doubled-up loose ends of the rope forming a large loop with which to pull it along.

"Ready?"

"Ready!"

Slowly but surely, they dragged the heavy chest all the way up the mountain slope to Duncan's cave. It took a long time with many breathers in between determined lugging to get it there, but it was too large to fit through the entrance gap to Duncan's living room, so they left it positioned as far as they could out of sight after pulling aside the piece of wooden fence behind the bush. Exhausted, they collapsed on the old settee to sleep.

"Tea?"

"What? Oh god yes! You're up early, Duncan?"

"Not really, it's about eleven," he said confidently without a clock in sight. "What do you reckon about those symbols in the upside-down triangle?"

"I think they're a clue to the numerical key to the combination lock. I know *pi* is 3.14159 to infinity, but I'll need to look up *e* and the other Greek letter. I'll make a copy of the plate engraving later, to take back with me. How about some breakfast, Duncan?"

"*Breakfast*? What do you think this place is? The Witch's Brew?"

Duncan later arrived around the corner of his cave with toast and marmalade and a steaming pot of tea, all produced in his corner kitchen over a robust fire set into a hollow in the rock floor and covered by an old piece of wire mesh.

*   *   *

A couple of hours later the professor was back in his room at the pub, with numbers – six needed digits – on his mind. He needed to make a telephone call. Eventually, George arrived with his groceries.

"Late today. Should have got this stuff first thing, but I got carried away clearing out the cellar."

"All those old bat and toad bits - eh! George. Can I borrow your phone?"

"Help yourself – I guess you'll leave me some pennies?"

"Well of course."

George fishes out the phone from beneath the bar, dumping it down with its bell dinging with disapproval at its rough treatment. The professor rumages in his wallet for a telephone number.

The Halloween Chamber

"Hello, it's Charlie Benson, could you put me through to the maths department, please?"

"*Well*, hello Charlie," said the surprised secretary. "Where *have* you been?"

"I'm on a job here in Scotland, Sally, trying to sort out some crazy monks at a spooky abbey."

"Are you having me on, Charlie?"

"No, *really* I am; but it's far more bizarre than you can imagine."

"OK, but you'll promise to tell me all about it when you get back? When *will* you be back?"

"Sometime at the beginning of November if all goes well; if it doesn't go well then probably never!"

"You're kidding! You take care of yourself, Charlie. Hang on and I'll put you through to Jenkins, he should be there at this time."

"Thanks, Sally."

After several attempts a breathless Doctor Jenkins speaks:

"Charlie . . . How're things?"

"Well, sort of OK - I need to pick your brain."

"Fire away."

"What is the first six digits of e?"

"Euler's number?"

"Is it?"

"Well, it usually is, Charlie. Give me a minute – I can't remember it off the top of my head. Two point something . . ."

The sound of frantic page turning ensued, with the professor toying with a shirt button in anticipation.

"Here it is!" Doctor Jenkins announced triumphantly, " . . . it's . . . have you got a pencil handy?"

"Yes, and paper!"

"2.7182818 - is that enough decimal places?"

The Halloween Chamber

"That's it! I only need the first six digits including the integer. Now, what's the symbol like a squiggly **Y**, but has a loop from the right hand fork?"

"A squiggly **Y**? No wonder you're not a maths guy! Sounds like a lower case *phi*."

"OK, *phi*. What's its value?"

"It's the Golden Ratio, Charlie, 1.618033; remember it as beginning sixteen eighteen."

"OK, thanks, and can you remind me of the value of *pi*."

"3.14159, that's to your six digits - not rounded. Can I ask why you want to know all this?"

"It's a puzzle to me at the moment, quite literally, so I'll let you know when I get back. Thanks again, and my regards to the family. Cheerio."

At last he had some numbers to play with, but had forgotten to ask Doctor Jenkins about the significance of the symbols being arranged in an inverted triangle. Then he remembered the Ohm's Law Triangle, even though it is right side up with a single vertex at the top.

V at the top and **I** and **R** at the bottom: **V** over **I** x **R**.

Although in Ohm's Law **V** = **I** x **R** it could be a clue in the triangle with the top portion being the dividend and the bottom portion the divisor. The diagram on the brass plate had φe at the top with π at the bottom.

So, φ times *e* divided by π equals:

1.61803 x 2.71828 ÷ 3.14159 = 1.40001

Was *this* the combination number? **1 4 0 0 0 1**

With the number jotted down on a slip of paper, the professor clambered back up to Duncan's cave the next day, always on the look-out for the lethal Thomas and Gregory.

The two eager men knelt by the chest with the professor clutching his piece of paper, hoping he did the arithmetic correctly.

The brass combination lock had ten positions for each of six rotary, milled-edged adjusters. The professor called out the numbers and Duncan dialed them in. With his hand on the sturdy clasp he levered it upwards and it opened, much to both their amazement.

"No! . . . You're a genius prof!" exploded Duncan.

"Just pure luck I got it right first time - *I* can't believe it either."

Tentatively they lifted the creaking oak lid to reveal a large number of beige linen bags.

"My goodness, these bags are heavy!" exclaimed the professor as he pulled on the tie ribbons, hardly able to control his excited expectation as to their contents. He walked over to Duncan's only carpet and put his hand under the first bag and tipped it over, with Duncan holding the torch.

Out tumbled hundreds of silver rings. They were the same as the ring Rose had shown him – SS Death's Head honour rings, SS – Ehrenring or *Totenkopfring*, which had gone missing from Himmler's Wewelsburg Castle at the end of the war. Here they were.

Some of the rings were inscribed inside with the name of an individual SS officer, his number and the date, together with Himmler's familiar jagged signature; the others were blank inside.

"Well, well, would you believe it."

"I had a hunch we might hit the jackpot with that chest, Duncan."

But Duncan didn't know anything about Nazi SS rings or German castles – not many did. But the professor did.

The Halloween Chamber

Underneath around a dozen ring bags was a folded uniform with the name Hans Kammler sewn into it, a Luger pistol with ammunition, and in a tin, SS badges and insignia. In a box was his peaked officer's hat emblazened with both a zinc eagle with swaztika beneath and a Death's Head skull.

"Well, now we know who abbot Gregory *really* is."

"Incredible that all this should be here so far from Germany. What shall we do with it all and the knowledge that this Nazi guy Kammler escaped from Germany?"

"We'll keep it all here, at least until after Halloween and then we'll have a rethink. We can hide them in one of your smaller caves."

"I know just the place – dry, where I keep my books."

The Halloween Chamber

CHAPTER FIFTEEN

Die Haunebu Glocke

With the summer months coming to a close, the professor and Rose spent many hours together, mainly in the privacy of her cottage. Even though the villagers knew of their friendship it would have been difficult to conduct at his shared room at The Witch's Brew.

One such autumnal day when the professor was visiting Rose, there was a knock at the door just after mid-day. Rose answered the door to a very attractive young woman whose long blonde hair was tied back into a pony tail. She asked if she could speak with them about an urgent matter.

Rose sat her down in an armchair by the window and called upstairs for the professor. Once downstairs, he was concerned to see this unusual young woman apparently in a state of agitation. After the professor had introduced himself and Rose, she began her story:

"I'm so sorry to bother you, but I need to talk. I know about your work at the abbey and I need to tell you both what's going on, because I'm afraid for my life."

"Where have you come from and where do you live?" asked the professor in a calm, gentle voice.

"I have lived at the abbey for eight years now; I've come

from Germany," she explained in her distinct German accent.

"You must be the young lady occasionally spotted in the grounds?"

"I have to get out of there from time to time . . . away from the abbot."

"Don't worry, we know who the abbot *really* is. What is your name?"

"That's impossible! *How* do you know? My name is Maria, Maria Orsitsch. So you know about Hans?"

"I've been made aware of this SS officer, yes. So both of you escaped from Germany in 1945 and brought the rings with you?"

"I'm astonished you know this!"

"Detective work. So you're afraid of being found out, obviously; and what about Mr. Kammler?"

"He's as crazy as Himmler and believes he'll be saved by supernatural forces embodied in Vril."

"*Vril*? What's Vril?" asked Rose.

"We believe it's a universal force which can be tapped into for good or evil and can be used in all manner of different ways. The miasma emanating from the chamber below the mausoleum is Vril, and the chamber is the template for part of Himmler's castle tower crypt. The width of the chamber here is exactly the same as the inner circle in Wewelsburg Castle's north tower crypt. Hans was working on Hitler's secret propulsion projects for discs, or flying saucers as you call them," explained Maria.

"But they're not *real!*" commented the professor.

"Oh, but they *are*," Maria insisted indignantly. They are *very* real. That's how we escaped without being detected. Hans piloted the Haunebu disc and then dumped it into the sea, just off the coast here," she turned pointing to the cliffs.

"My god! So *that's* what they've discovered - a flying saucer!" realised the professor with a look of utter disbelief upon his face.

"We've known that the abbey was built on an ancient site for satanic worship called Grim's Fell, a place to conjure Vril from the underworld of the Dark Sun, and that here is the rightful place for us Aryan people; Oros mountain resembles Mount Elbrus, the sacred Aryan twin-peaked mountain in Russia.

"The ritual chamber was hewn out at the bottom of a well over the river tunnel in the old days to reach the Vril portal and was concealed by the building which eventually became the abbey mausoleum. The abbey itself was built much later as a convincing cover, but the monks didn't know that – just the ones affected by the power of Vril. Another Vril chamber was later built between the river tunnel and the abbey crypt dedicated to the Lords of the Black Stone, *Die Herren vom Schwarzen Stein*. Also, pure Vril is believed to be extracted by witches at the moment of a young child's death – their new life energy - but I don't know if this is true or not."

"Maria," interrupted the professor, "this is both fascinating and fantastical, but why have you chosen to tell us all this?"

"I feel guilty. Guilt because *I* found out about the power of Vril and how to make flying disc machines through being a medium – a channel to another race of people, far, far away. Many years later Rudolf Hess was with me in Munich when I again received information in a strange language by automatic writing; it turned out to be Sumerian and my friend was able to decipher it.

"Hess tried to reach sacred Grim's Fell too, but I understand he became lost when he was low on fuel looking for somewhere to land and crashed his plane. He had

The Halloween Chamber

convinced Hitler it was a peace mission to try and end the war by meeting Churchill through The Golden Dawn in Scotland. It's *all* my fault you see - *my* fault that these people attempted to use the power of Vril to defeat our enemies - an unstoppable power in its many forms.

"I escaped with Hans and we became lovers, but once here he seemed overwhelmed by the fact that he was at the magic place which Himmler had believed in; he was compelled to carry on the work after Himmler's suicide. Hitler's burnt body was faked with one of his doubles and he may still be alive, possibly in Argentina, to join with Hans again, now without Hess, to create their dream of the Fourth Reich."

"This is the truth, then," asks the professor. "What you are telling us *is the truth*? All this supernatural stuff sounds just too much to be believed, except I know through my own experience that it does seem to exist outside of our heads to have a real effect in the *real* world."

"I can't go back to the abbey . . . I'm frightened of Hans . . . Can you help me? I will tell you more . . . more about *Die Glocke* – The Bell."

"What bell is this, Maria?" Rose asks with a frown.

"It is an extremely large bell-shaped, very high speed centrifugal machine which forms the central hub of the newest flying discs; it was being tested when the war ended. The disc and crew canopy above was later attached to The Bell and named *Die Haunebu Glocke*. There's one over there," she glanced towards the coast. "Our escape turned out to be another test flight - in the dimensions of both space and time. I believe the other *Die Glocke* hubs and plans were destroyed to prevent them falling into foreign hands."

"What are we going to do with you, Maria?" sighed the professor.

"Another thing that greatly concerns me is that I haven't aged since contacting the Aldebarans. I fear I am immortal . . . I don't want to live forever. I'm fifty eight years old now and born on Halloween – that's another reason why both Himmler and Hess embraced the Vril as an absolute truth.

"The Vril miasma can escape from the underworld when the membrane separating it from the world above is at its thinnest on this date, *especially* in this special place. Demons are real and rupture the membrane accompanied by a terrible low frequency humming vibration which pulsates energetically, and it is this noise energy that breaks through the barrier into our world, created by the summoned demon. This satanic entity is the demonic manifestation of Vril itself; the other form is angelic. Vril, this volatile electric fluid, is polarised: malevolent and benevolent – the former attracted to those of evil intent and the latter for good.

"I'm very afraid that if Hitler *is* still alive and returns, and Hess escapes, they and Hans will find me and make me pay for what I have told you."

"Why do you affectionately refer to Kammler as Hans, Maria," asked Rose.

"Because, as I said, we were once close and I just always refer to him as Hans – I hate and fear the man really."

"How did Kammler disguise his German accent?" asked the professor.

"By many years of obsessional training; he felt it essential if he needed to escape here – to Britain."

"Well, he did a damned good job of it I must say. Is that thing in the sea radioactive?"

"Only inside the sealed Bell where the thorium and red mercury is held, but it has massively thick ceramic and iron walls and is designed to be as safe as possible . . . except it *wasn't* safe – too many people died beside it during testing and more *wissenschaftler* perished later - murdered to protect the secret knowledge from the enemy.

"The Bell was built to produce fissionable uranium 233 for a nuclear bomb, but it was discovered that the great speed of the spinning twin-cylinder centrifuge generated its own independent space-time field together with the very high voltage magnetic field, so it was incorporated into the disc craft, the Haunebu, for experiments as a space *and time* travel vehicle."

Maria explained the design and position of three other domed drive components hanging beneath the craft, doubling as a landing tripod.

"There is one other last secret . . . but I can't tell you that."

"Intriguing, Maria; perhaps one day?"

"Perhaps."

"Maria, how do you know all these technical scientific terms about centrifuges and flying saucers?" asked Rose.

"Hans would speak of little else – he is obsessional about it."

"Well, you'll have to stay here with me for the time being, at least until we know where we all stand after . . . well . . . after your birthday, because that's when we plan to kill the Bennett corvids who summon the demon to perpetuate their annual production of the evil miasma – the Vril, as you call it. We will end their eternal pursuit of revenge once and for all during those brief precious minutes when they become mortal."

"Thank you, Rose. What can I do to help with your mission to try and end all this evil?"

"Keep the home fires burning on the day, Maria."

CHAPTER SIXTEEN

Preparation

At long last the wait was nearly over. October 30th had arrived and the group met at mid-day in The Witch's Brew. George had prepared food and drink for everyone which would sustain them until the job was done. Rose looked particularly nervous which prompted the professor to again enquire if she wanted to go ahead and accompany them on the mission.

"We can manage without you, Rose, if you'd rather not come along," he said quietly.

"Charlie, if there's something in this life I *must* do, it is this: to see an end to this reign of terror perpetrated by my ancestors. We simply *must* succeed and I must be there to witness it."

"I do understand," he said sympathetically, placing his hand comfortingly on her shoulder, "just as long as you're sure you can cope. It will be a hazardous journey to the Chamber along the river tunnel, and then goodness knows what will happen."

"I know . . . but I have to see it through, Charlie."

George poured out the drinks and gestured for the others

to help themselves to food and then pulled out a scruffy piece of paper from his equally scruffy jacket pocket and scrutinised it.

"What've you got there, George?" commented Gail.

"My notes and concerns," he mumbled whilst chewing away on his bread.

"We're *all* concerned, George, but so much is an unknown at this stage that it's pointless worrying about it. What we must do is put our trust in our final decision as to how we'll dispose of the Bennett siblings once they regain human form in that evil stone chamber. Fire is the best option then - we're sure about that?"

"Not sure, Gail, but fairly certain. Brother Dawson and I have tested all the oxygen masks."

"And I've checked the oxygen cylinders again," added the professor. "They're not too big, but heavy and entirely necessary. The fire will quickly use up the oxygen in that confined space, but the river tunnel should be fine."

"We must try to kill them *before* they conjure up that damn demon or we'll all risk being swiftly satanised too," Gail added.

"That's a good word . . . well, an *evil* word," said George.

"We've carefully planned this for months," said the professor. "There's nothing more we can do, unless that is, anyone has any ideas? We can only hope the rain stays off as that river will become a raging torrent in next to no time."

The room fell silent, but outside the wind howled, filling them all with a sense of foreboding for what exactly the next day had in store for them.

Duncan stood up. "We must be on our way early this evening. We can't afford to miss mid-day tomorrow and we don't know exactly how long their nasty little ritual will last.

The Halloween Chamber

We have to catch them with the flame-throwers when they're vulnerable – at the moment they completely return to human form."

Duncan knew the tunnels and cave system of Oros better than anyone, and again went through the tunnel plan on the table before them.

"Right, a bit of geology!" he began. "This is where I live, in one of the bigger caves inside the mountain. All of this system was at one time flooded and the limestone gradually eroded away over millions of years by flowing acidified water to form the tunnels and caves."

Duncan traces the route on his map with his finger.

"So, we can navigate from my cave down to The Halloween Chamber under the mausoleum; to the abbey crypt chamber, and finally down, and then up, into the Witch's Cave under Lovers' Crag as the plan B escape route. We've only one chance this year and we need to access the Chamber stealthily by the tunnel for the element of surprise."

"Is there a chance they'll see or hear us at the Chamber's river entrance," Gail asks.

"Almost impossible; I've been there twice myself. Once in position and the ritual begun, they're oblivious to everything around them, and *that's* when they're vulnerable; they can't hear much anyway above the sound of the rushing water. The prof and I will lead, then we'll fire up the throwers at the right moment, if that's all right with you?" he said turning to the professor who nodded, looking worried at the prospect.

"Have we a back-up if the throwers don't work?" queried Rose.

"No. Only intense fire will end their immortality – sort of like creating a small fiery Hell to merge them back into the real place they belong. My presence there will only stop the demon if I call upon the power, but it could revert them back to those immortal birds before the fire does its job and we can't risk that."

"How do you know it'll work, Duncan?" said a worried Gail.

"The short answer is, I don't." This did not inspire confidence. "It's the best I can come up with; you'll just have to trust me."

Evening arrived all too soon as the six members of the assassination team carrying all their equipment, climbed up to the base of the mountain the long way, by-passing the abbey and cutting across well behind the mausoleum to Duncan's secret cave entrance and through into his living room.

After resting, some top-up food and drink and the occasional nap, they again checked the torches, oxygen masks and cylinders, ropes and their watches. The flame-throwers had been tested earlier in the day behind the pub, much to the excitement of the local children who thought bonfire night had arrived seven days early!

"I reckon it'll take half an hour or so to reach the Chamber from the river tunnel entrance below here, and about ten minutes to set up the equipment, so we'll leave here at eleven tomorrow," Duncan decided. "Termination Day has finally arrived."

CHAPTER SEVENTEEN

Confrontation

Deep beneath Duncan's living room a passageway led down to the river tunnel. Duncan led the way followed by the professor along the rocky tunnel floor, swirling with crystal clear water about a foot deep, each person lighting the way with a powerful torch; the two women were next in line with George and Brother Dawson following.

On Duncan's second visit to The Halloween Chamber he had marked the wall at every thirty steps – passing fifty markers would place them at the Chamber's entrance.

"That's twenty five markers; did you make it that, prof?" asked Duncan.

"Twenty five it is – half way."

Then, just beyond the forty fifth marker, above the sound of the rushing water, they heard the echoing chatter of the corvids further down the tunnel as they arrived at the Chamber from the Witch's Cave, as they had done at this time every year for centuries.

"That's a scary sound if ever I heard one," remarked Gail.

With just over forty yards to go, the noise of the evil birds became overwhelming as the excitement of their anticipation at regaining their human form once again became imminent. Soon, their frenetic flapping shadows were visible to the group on the far side tunnel wall opposite the Chamber entrance, projected by the dim light emanating from its roof well shaft opening through the mausoleum wall, as mid-day approached high above. With hushed voices, the group replayed their well-practiced routine of preparing the flame-throwers for action and putting on their oxygen masks.

"How long before they settle down into their positions, Duncan?"

"It's now ten minutes to mid-day when the portal opens, so it won't be long, prof."

Soon after that, the Chamber fell silent and Duncan held out a small mirror to see what was happening. The corvids had positioned themselves at the bottom of the four alcoves and had become almost comatose with concentration as they directed their collective minds to summon the Demon of Revenge to tear through the membrane separating their two worlds.

Duncan signalled to the others to be ready on the valves as they took positions to one side of the entrance. Rumblings could be felt through the rocky floor, increasing in intensity to a terrible pulsating drone resonating throughout the tunnel.

"What's that god-awful noise, Duncan?" asked an anxious Gail.

"Oh! I didn't tell you about that – it's the demon on its way."

"We've heard that sound before in the village on Halloween – we *thought* it must be coming up through the ground."

"In other parts of the world it's commonly called the *Devil's Drone*," added Duncan, "and not only on Halloween!"

"You mean there are *other* portals?"

"Too many – you wouldn't believe it. But that's another story."

A faint whisp of greenish-grey miasma appeared through the floor's central aperture, quickly becoming an upward streaming plume of filth. Inhaling deeply, the corvids violently shuddered as their bodies morphed from avian to human form, gradually increasing with size until they eventually filled their alcoves.

The miasma quickly changed into the form of the chosen demon as it became more solid in form, changing to a deep olive. The Bennetts blinked across at each other and Daniel spoke:

"We meet again brothers and sister."

Alice was a haggard, stooping crone whose stony jet black evil eyes glanced from one brother to the next. The three brothers acknowledged their sister's presence.

"Welcome sister," they uttered, one after the other as the demon suddenly disintegrated into billions of miasmids – each an evil entity with the power to transmit and infect satanic insanity to their hosts, like some airborne virus.

The team were taken by surprise at the unexpected pace of events. Masked and ready, the professor, Duncan and Brother Dawson took up their preplanned positions just inside the entrance with the weapons' pilot lights lit; George and the two women stood ready to take their place when their tanks were emptied.

"Now!" yelled Duncan, as nervous fingers pulled at the valves releasing a maelstrom of streaming fire directly at the Bennett siblings. Unable to move amidst their ritual summoning of the demon, their tortured screams of human mortality echoed around The Halloween Chamber. The copious production of miasmids had already flowed out past the team and on down the river tunnel to beneath the abbey, as the hideous, haunting pulsing drone which had shaken their body organs finally faded away.

The widened eyes of the screaming, flailing Bennetts reflected their horror at the fiery onslaught as the remaining three assassins took over to finally reduce them to the steaming blood of cooking living meat, as thick black grease, the very essence of their evil, accumulated and drained down the Chamber walls to pool in a syrup-like slurry around their collapsed and charred remains.

Stepping back from their successful task into the mountain side of the tunnel entrance, they became aware that the flames had ignited the demon's volatile outpouring of miasmids and had flashed down the tunnel to beneath the abbey. The screams of the now deceased Bennett clan were replaced by the sound of hissing gases escaping their blackened distorted corpses and the cracking of bones.

Duncan frantically gesticulated for everyone to retreat back up the tunnel the way they had come. Without the oxygen masks and cylinders they would not have survived. Thankful the oxygen hadn't ignited in their masks they were able to move faster without the now abandoned heavy flame-throwers. The women and Brother Dawson led the way back to Duncan's cave with a blaze of triumphant torchlight.

Grimsfell abbey erupted violently in flames as the burning miasmids travelled up through the ancient wooden shafts once used to bucket-haul water from the river below. Being mid-day, almost everyone was assembled in the dining hall next to vast opening windows, much loved in the summer time and looking out from the side of this more recent addition to the abbey built after the original fire. All escaped to stand and watch the abbey's fiery demise. The old part of the abbey with its library, which had survived the ancient fire, was now, in its turn, being consumed.

Kammler and his accomplice Thomas weren't so lucky. They were high above on the abbey roof planning how to dispose of the professor and Brother Dawson. Kammler, wearing his raven robes, was convinced of his powers which he believed gave him an overwhelming advantage of immortality over those without the special powers endowed upon him from the dark side. *His beloved Vril was about to kill him.*

He was last seen from below by the assembled monks and village workers as he was consumed by flames igniting the very feathered robes he thought would protect him from harm. This time, his energetic flapping only fanned the flames hastening his end and afforded him no flight as he plummeted earthwards to a sickening end. The evil Thomas was never found.

The exhausted team spent time recovering with the welcome addition of a Duncan tea brew-up special, illuminated by the remaining torchlight. No one knew the abbey was burning. Gail returned after hoping for a breath of fresh air outside the cave entrance.

"There's an awfully strong smell of smoke out there. Do you think the old well at the Chamber acted as a chimney?"

"Very likely," agreed Duncan.

The weary but happy group eventually made their way back down to the abbey, soon aware of the source of the smoke. The abbey was well alight with the entire population of Grimswell in attendance. It soon became apparent that the burning evil miasmic Vril had travelled all the way into the

The Halloween Chamber

depths of the abbey, this time devouring itself along with its abbey host instead of infecting it.

Cheers and clapping greeted the returned heroes and they were told of the bizarre event of a man dressed as a raven who had fallen screaming from the roof. The crowd had dragged his body away from the flames and extinquished his feathered robe. Charlie Benson knew who it was.

Pulling away the smoking monstrous raven-beaked headpiece revealed a very dead Hans Kammler a.k.a. Abbot Gregory.

Back at The Witch's Brew, an excited Maria approached the professor.

"Now I know Hans Kammler is dead, I want to tell you about the last secret I mentioned back at Rose's house; in fact there are two."

"Shall we talk in my room, Maria?"

"Yes, of course."

The professor excuses the untidy room he has shared with Brother Dawson over the months and clears an armchair.

"Hitler escaped with us in the Bell Haunebu and stayed for some years hiding in the abbey attic before he dare venture out. He was going mad and felt trapped, so he grew his hair and beard long to disguise his features and spent his time exploring the villages around here."

"But you said he was headed for Argentina."

"That was a cover. It was the very place he was expected to have gone because of all the Nazi sympathisers and Peron, so he decided to come with us."

"My goodness! You're certainly full of surprises, Miss Orsitsch. So, Adolf Hitler is here with us – where exactly?"

"I don't know, professor; he's become a recluse somewhere

nearby because he occasionally visited the abbey to see Hans and I, although he spoke very little to me."

"What is the second secret, Maria?"

"He brought the Grail with him – the famed Holy Grail, at least he was utterly convinced it was."

"What exactly is this object? I think of it as a chalice."

"It is simply a large black stone or crystal which has very powerful magical properties; I think of it as a solid, condensed form of Vril."

"So he carries this around with him then?"

"No, it was hidden inside the black altar in the chamber behind the abbey crypt."

"How do you know this, Maria?"

"I was there."

Other books by Richard E Harding
Available on Amazon

CRYPTIC VISIONS : The Summerhouse Project

A story of international Cold War treachery and murder, from Washington DC and New York to London and Moscow.

Acting on images collected from the mind of a comatose special agent, a young doctor and nurse team in the 1980s undertake the perilous task of trying to prevent the Cold War from turning into World War Three, as unknowingly, the two superpowers take the world to the brink of Armageddon.

The supernatural ambience of a derelict Victorian summerhouse in an English garden holds the memories and secrets of illicit passionate love.

A LIFE IN TORMENT : Enduring a Lifetime of OCD

The author graphically describes in painful detail what it is like to be constantly controlled by severe, unrelenting obsessive-compulsive behaviour from many aspects of his life: from childhood with an anxious mother, through school and into employment and marriage, at a time when OCD was virtually undocumented. Sixty plus continuous years of torment unfolded.

Only later did he realise that he may have Asperger's Syndrome, which explained his obsession with detail and love of complicated subjects, as well as the strong and dark OCD component of his AS.

Proof

Made in the USA
Charleston, SC
26 April 2016